KELLIE TAYLOR HALL

authorHOUSE®

AuthorHouse™
1663 Liberty Drive
Bloomington, IN 47403
www.authorhouse.com
Phone: 1 (800) 839-8640

Noel Malfe as front cover artist

Published by AuthorHouse 01/31/2017

ISBN: 978-1-5246-5954-7 (sc)
ISBN: 978-1-5246-5953-0 (e)

Library of Congress Control Number: 2017900471

Print information available on the last page.

This book is printed on acid-free paper.

Acknowledgement

Since this is my first attempt at writing a book, I have had to recruit several people to help. I would like to take this opportunity to thank them for all of their support during this novice writing experience. First, I would like to thank my family. Thank you for all of the encouragement that you have bestowed on me during this adventure. Thank you for offering your opinions whenever I was indecisive and just needed your input. I would especially like to thank my daughter, Falon, for her opinion on some of the text and for answering the phone, no matter what time early in the morning representatives from Author House called.

Next, I would like to thank my friend and colleague, Carly Adderholt, for her encouragement and enthusiasm. You helped pep me up when the stress of this endeavor was pulling me down. I also want to thank you and your daughter, Caycie Adderholt, for helping me with word choice in those few instances when I knew what I wanted to say but the word was just not coming to me. Even though Caycie is only four years old, she was right there giving her two cents as well.

In addition, I wish to give a special thanks to another friend and colleague, Tracey McWhorter-Gossett, for helping with my photography questions. My motto is when you don't know the answer go to someone that does and you were that person for me. Thank you for your patience and willingness to help, including helping me find a local artist to help with the cover of my book.

Thank you Noel Malfe for painting the cover for my book. Thank you for your excitement and willingness to work with me on this project. Thank you for the great work you produced and for handling my critiques when the design was not exactly what I wanted. You were a great person with whom to collaborate. Thank you for showing patience when I wasn't even sure what I wanted and then putting my eventual ideas on paper.

Furthermore, I would like to thank my Author House project representatives, Rowella Alvaro, Toni Arkins, and Leigh Allen, for helping me through the process and making the eventual publication of my book possible.

Finally, I would like to thank all of the past, present and future students of Ringgold High School for inspiring me to step out of my comfort zone and write a novel just for you. I encourage you all to find a book of interest and read, just make sure you include my book in that repertoire.

Prologue

Looking up into the gray sky, Caya Braswell felt the pelting of rain drops beating her face. *This rain is running down my jacket and onto my legs. I have goose bumps the size of baseballs. I can't believe I let James talk me into hiking when the clouds looked like they would provide us with a deluge any second. It rarely rains in this part of Washington State, but let me get outside for the day and the heavens open and present us with liquid sunshine.* "Caya get the move on before we become water logged out here and James and Lars throw us in a dryer at the laundry mat." "Please quit with the drama Rayna. These rocks are slick. Do you want me to slide off a cliff?" *This is so not my thing. I would rather be curled up in my cushiony recliner with a good romance novel letting the heroine participate in the outdoor adventures.*

Caya was picking her way through the rocky terrain with the utmost care. James was just a head of her but had slowed so that she could catch up to him. "Let's wait for Caya to catch up with us. Don't rush babe. Rayna you are going to make her slide on these rocks." "James I can't believe that you talked her into coming. You know she doesn't like hiking, especially in the rain. Whose idea was this anyway, yours' or Lars'?" Rayna was just as drenched as everyone else. She was struggling with the idea of waiting on her best friend or seeking shelter. "Lars, honey, I can't stand another minute out in this waterfall." Rayna's words were drowned out by a loud clap of thunder that persuaded Rayna to make a decision to seek shelter immediately. "James we are running to the truck. Stay and wait on your girlfriend."

Rayna and I have been roommates and best friends since college. How can she just run off and leave me out here? She's already drenched anyway what is another stitch of clothing going to matter. These rocks feel like I am ice skating. My feet are sliding like a fawn trying to walk for the first time. "James I am freezing how much further until we make it to the truck?" "Caya you are doing great. Don't let Rayna get your dander up and make you hurry. We don't have much further. We have two more big rocks to get over and we will have flat land all the way to our ride."

Great!!! My lungs feel like a blazing furnace, my clothes are clinging to me like Saranwrap, and I can no longer feel my feet and legs, but I am doing great. I can't believe my traitorous best friend has abandoned me. If she thinks I am going to proofread anymore papers for her she has another thing coming. Finally, surely I can get past the last boulder for today. Suddenly, Caya's foot is sliding on a huge bolder as if she were skating on glass. Her butt makes contact with said glass and she is sliding down this monstrosity of a rock. "James!" James hears Caya yell and turns to see her sliding on her butt down the rock, barreling for the edge of the cliff.

Chapter 1

Four Weeks Later

Spring has sprung around the Puyallup River. There will be a plethora of daffodils for sale this year. The yellow trumpets have just opened turning the ground into a beautiful, floral painting. James, Caya, Rayna, and Lars are picnicking along the river bank enjoying the picturesque view of Mount Rainier, in the distance, and the hills through which the river travels. Lars whispers in Rayna's ear, "I can't believe he got her back out in the wild." Rayna was quick to reply, "What do you think he promised her Lars?" "Who knows what he has up his sleeve. Perhaps he enticed her with the beautiful scenery and the fact that the sun is shining this time." Caya noticed Lars and Rayna in secret conversation. "What are you two contemplating this time?" Rayna just shrugs and smiles.

As the sun sinks lower in the sky, Caya and Rayna start packing up the day's equipment as the guys finish their attempt at catching fish for dinner. Caya is daydreaming as she listens to the lapping of the water over the rocks on the bank. She is shaken from her reverie by a feeling she can't describe. It is like eyes are burrowing into her back and making her feel uneasy. She turns to see a group of young people heading toward her. There are four strapping young men taking in the scenery as well. They appear to be in their mid to late twenties. The one leading the pack is staring at her as though he could see right into her soul. He has eyes the color of emeralds. Caya had never seen eyes so green. His hair is brown with auburn highlights. Even with his emerald gems boring into her eyes, she is not afraid. As a matter of fact, she is drawn to him. Not only can she not tear her eyes away from his, but she feels like she belongs to him. His body is perfectly sculpted under his tight t-shirt and his jeans look like they were made just for him. The attraction seems to be mutual, but it also seems there is more between them.

Caya recognizes a presence that has just appeared at her side, James. He snakes his arm around her waist as if to advertise his possession of her. Caya starts shaking uncontrollably. Her temperature has risen what feels like a 100 degrees as she feels the sweat sliding down her forehead. *What is wrong with me? It's like I have never seen a good looking guy.*

The guys stop thirty feet in front of Caya. Lars has sent Rayna back to the truck with some of the provisions as the newcomers approach. "My name is Nick," says the guy whose eyes are still pinned to Caya. "I know who you are. I am James and this is Lars." "This is Seth, and his brother Aaron. You know that you are in our territory and you are required to notify us in advance," says Nick who is briefly meeting James' gaze, but quickly returning his sights on Caya. "We are just tourists from Tacoma sightseeing and enjoying the beauty of the mountain and river. We are no threat," says James stiffening and tightening his hold on Caya. "Why is he talking as if we are trespassing?" asks Caya, her eyes still on Nick. James realizes he has tightened his grip on Caya and lets his arm loosen around her as he says, "There is nothing to worry about honey. We are leaving anyway." Caya starts shaking again and she feels tiny pin pricks all over her skin, which is still radiating heat. Her head is starting to pound as she looks at her right arm and then her left and realizes she has sprouted an abundance of fur on them. Caya screams, "No! What is happening to me?" James tells Caya not to panic as Nick comes and helps James lower her to the ground. Nick's glance toward James shows consternation. James explains, "She is new at this." Nick asks, "You mean she has never changed?"

James whispers in Caya's ear, "Just breathe honey. I know it is scary, but don't lose yourself. Concentrate on my voice and stay with me." "I think she is going into shock and she is only going to complete the change if we don't think of something fast," deduces Nick. Nick felt the connection as soon as he exited his truck. Once he was bombarded with the realization, he couldn't help but seek her out. When they made eye contact for the first time, he knew he would never let her leave him. He could tell by her reaction that she felt it as well. The biggest obstacle was to get her away from this other male who thought he had claims on her. He had no time to sugar coat what he was about to reveal. She needed him to react immediately. James was on one side and Nick on the other as they eased her ever so carefully to the ground.

Nick interjected, "She and I have a strong connection. She is my mate. Let me rein her in as her Alpha." James' face is pinched as he says, "Your mate! Who do you think you are? She is my girlfriend. You stay away from her." Seth and Aaron close rank around their Alpha as Lars does the same to James. Thinking quickly, Nick adds, "We can't let anyone see her change James. We cannot expose our packs to those who would be threatened by our kind. Caya you need to listen to your Alpha and subdue your wolf." Caya's eyes are filled with fear as she opens her mouth to say, "My w-o-l-f?" Nick speaks to her in quiet tones, hoping to soothe her. Nick has no idea why Caya, a grown woman, has never changed, but he doesn't have time to contemplate it now. "I know you don't understand what is happening to your body, but I must speak to your wolf. I am her Alpha and she will listen to me. "Stay hidden wolf. It is not your time to appear. Back down and relinquish control to Caya, now!"

Caya's shaking lessens as does the hammer in her head. Gradually, her arms return to normal, human arms. She realizes she is still rather warm as she faints. Lars goes to get water from the river to wipe across her face. The water soaked shirt is cool as James wipes Caya's face and neck. Caya awakes to see all of these men peering down at her. "I think I am losing my mind!" explodes Caya. "Caya, I can explain, but we need to get you home," acquiesces James. Nick realizes he must make a move before he loses his mate to this rival wolf. "You are not taking my mate anywhere!" thunders Nick.

James knows he has to do something to get Caya away from this Alpha, but he doesn't have a clue what to do. He is scrambling for some reason to insist the leader is wrong about his connection with Caya. "Nick, she is my girlfriend who has just had a huge scare. She doesn't even know you. There is no way she is going to go anywhere with *you*," counters James. "Caya you must make a decision. I know that you are confused about your change, but I can tell that you feel the connection that we have between us. I would never hurt you. I will protect you. I will help you through this change. It will happen again. You need your Alpha to help you through this transition. If you can't decide to return with me to my home, let the wolf inside you guide you. She will always protect you and have your best interest at heart. Do you feel threatened by me?" asked Nick.

Caya looked into those emerald orbs and felt a sense of safety and something else, something she had never felt before, longing. After several long minutes, Caya replied, "No, I don't feel threatened, but I am very scared and confused by what is happening to me. You were able to help me stop it Nick and for that I am thankful." She wondered if her confusion was guiding her decision or if it was as Nick implied, her wolf. James noticed how she grabbed Nick's arm before looking at him and giving her response, "James I feel like I need to go with Nick. I need to get this under control. If I am like him, he may be able to help me." James couldn't believe what he was hearing, even though he knew if Caya and Nick felt this connection they really could be mates. How would he ever live with that?

I love Caya. I can't stand to see her leave with this wolf hero. However, Caya needs someone who can bring comfort to her during her transition. I was not able to do that just a few minutes ago. I must think of what is best for her. I will convince her that they are not mates, that he is just taking advantage of her in her weakened state. "Caya are you saying you want to leave with Nick?" She wasted no time with her reply, "James, I don't want to hurt you, but I feel like he can help me. Please let him try." James balls his hands into fists as he says, "Ok, but Nick, if she asks to come back home at any point, you must let her return to me." Nick places his large hand on Caya's shoulder and uses his other hand to lift her from under her arm. Just his touch sends a different pin prick throughout her body.

Her thoughts returned to her friend, "James, don't tell Rayna what happened to me. I don't want her to know. Tell her that I am sick. I don't want to endanger any of you. What if I turn into a wolf and go on a killing spree? What if I don't remember who my friends are?" Although Caya's reaction should not have surprised James, it did. It took him a minute to reply, "Caya you are still you and you are not going to kill innocent people." Caya shoots back, "How do you know I won't become some sadistic monster?" "Caya, I know because all of us standing around you are werewolves," James states carefully, but matter of fact. "What!" Caya screams for the second time.

Chapter 2

Nick, Seth, and Aaron are on either side of Caya as they leave the Puyallup River and make their way toward Nick's truck. Caya can feel the heat coming off of Nick even though he has put a little air between them as they walk. Caya is deep in thought as they travel the mile to the parking lot. *Could Nick really be the same animal that I am since I can feel the heat from his body when he isn't even touching me or is this just some infatuation I have with him? No way, I do not believe in love at first sight. Whatever is happening to my body must be affecting my hormones. I would never leave my boyfriend and follow some hunk I just met by a river. Who does that? This is it. The stress of teaching has finally caught up with me and I have lost my mind after only three years in the profession. Who are these people and why are they calling themselves werewolves when I plainly recognize them as human beings? Well, there is the matter of the hair that I saw growing on my arms. Was that just a delusion of grandeur or did it really happen? I am always the safe, practical one or at least I have been for the first quarter of my life. I should be totally afraid of these men who are escorting me to parts unknown, but strangely, I am perfectly at ease with them, like I belong with them. I am definitely having some kind of delusion.*

Nick brings Caya back to reality by stating, "That's my truck, the black Dodge Ram." He opens the passenger side door and places his hand under her arm to give her assistance into the truck. *Werewolves don't drive trucks, right? They run on all fours, no need for transportation. I was hearing things earlier when they claimed they were werewolves. What about the fur on my arms? It always comes back to that.* "Caya I am going to take you back to my pack and we have a great doctor who will check you out," replied Nick as his face and then his neck started turning bright red. "I mean that he will do some tests and make sure you are overall healthy. Don't be afraid. I will explain what is going on with your body and what to expect when you change. I will be there to help you through all of it. I hope you will trust me." Caya, who has been staring out the windshield thus far, turned to look at Nick. She noticed his tightened jaw, his bright eyes, the death grip he had on the steering wheel and yet for all of his nervous, stressed appearance, she felt rather calm. Well, as calm as one could be when she saw fur growing on her arms and knew she was going to change into a werewolf at some point. She faced the front again and all she could say was, "Ok. Why do you call your home a pack?" Nick briefly took his eyes off the road to look at her. "I call them a pack because that is what we are.

We are a pack of wolves. We are family. We are your family now. You will be part of our pack." His eyes returned to the road as Caya replied, "So you are kidnapping me." Nick let out a sigh. Seth and Aaron snicker from the back seat. "No, we are not kidnapping you. Remember you chose to come with us, willingly." Caya didn't miss the subtle irritation that came with that remark. "What if I decide that I don't like your pack or **you** for that matter?" His irritation was only growing stronger, Nick dictates, "You are my mate. I understand you do not understand what that means right now, but you will. You know you feel an attraction, a connection with me. That is because you are my mate. You will learn in time that that connection will make it impossible for you to leave me. It will only distress you if we are separated." Caya's anger came to the forefront of the conversation. "Who do you think you are God's gift to woman? Do you think you can just take any she-wolf for your mate?" Vehemence was radiating from his mate and Nick could feel it through their connection. He tried to calm her again through their connection as he did by the river when she was trying to change for the first time. This was not how he wanted the conversation to go. This was his first encounter with a mate. He was treading in new territory and he wasn't sure how to navigate it. It was working. He could feel her wolf reacting to his Alpha power. She was starting to relax again.

Why has she never changed? Is something wrong with her wolf? I have got to get her to Dr. Hill and let him shed some light on her inability to change prior to now. Caya thought Nick's quiet demeanor was because she had pushed him to his breaking point. She thought she had made him angry. *What happens when you confront an angry wolf who is in his human form?* The alleged kidnapper spoke, "I only profess to be your mate. You will understand in time what being one's mate entails." He seemed calm but sure when he made this statement. They turned off onto a dirt road that snaked through the woods for close to two miles. Nick pulled the truck up to a whitewashed building with a red, metal roof. Seth interrupted Caya's thoughts, "Nick, Aaron and I will go to our families if you think you can handle it from here." Nick turned off the truck and rotated to face Seth in the back seat. "I have it. I'll see you in my office in the morning at the regular time." *Apparently, the entertainment was over and Seth and Aaron were getting out of Dodge before the conversation between the mates became anymore heated*, thought Caya. Nick helped her out of the truck and escorted her to the red roof building without touching her, giving her the space he thought she needed. Nick introduced Caya to Dr. Hill and indicated that Caya should have a seat in the gray, cushioned, office chair to her right. Caya sat while Nick ushered Dr. Hill to what appeared to be an office a few steps away from Caya. They didn't shut the door, but they were speaking in hushed voices and she couldn't hear what was being said.

Caya felt her palms become sweaty as Nick and the doctor returned to her. Nick said, "Caya, Dr. Hill is going to evaluate you. I trust him implicitly as should you. I have to check in at my home while you are undergoing the evaluation. I am in no way abandoning you. I will be here waiting when you return. Will you be ok?" Caya looked at him with a puzzled expression. "You kidnap me and then pawn me off on some other man in less than an hour?" Nick looked at Dr. Hill as he spoke. "Caya, we have already established that you have not been kidnapped. You came here willingly and I am certainly not pawning you off, as you say, on anyone. You are my sole responsibility and I would not leave you with anyone I didn't trust. Would you feel more comfortable if I sat here and waited? I can make phone calls if I can't check on things in person." Caya was reluctant to let Nick leave her. Although they had just met, he made her feel safe. He also irritated her with his, "I am your mate," mumbo jumbo. "No, you can go attend to your business. I am sure that Dr. Hill will do his best to evaluate me to his fullest ability." "Are you sure?" Nick asked reluctantly. "Yes, go before I change my mind."

Dr. Hill led the patient down to an examining room via a hallway that smelled of strong disinfectant. Like the hallway, the room smelled very sterile. There was a hospital bed rather than a gurney, which made her feel a little more comfortable. The walls were of a pale, yellow hue. It reminded her of the color of the daffodils that she had admired earlier that day. Dr. Hill left her to change into a hospital gown. As she changed into the gown, she closed her eyes and imagined the hissing of the river, the beautiful daffodils, and the majestic mountain. She felt herself calming. The doctor returned with a clipboard and asked her questions for no less than thirty minutes. He sent a nurse in to take some blood. Neither he nor the nurse looked like werewolves. After two hours of being questioned, poked and prodded, the nurse left her to change into her street clothes. She was expecting the doctor to return to tell her there was some misunderstanding and she had imagined the fur covered extremities, and that she was completely human.

When the nurse came back to escort her back to the waiting area, Caya was perplexed. "Isn't Dr. Hill going to come give me the results of all of my tests?" Caya asked. The nurse indicated that she should follow her to the waiting area where as promised Nick sat waiting. He smiled and Caya thought she could get lost in that smile. It was a distinct contradiction to the scowl he had on his visage as they had their heated conversation on the way here. "Have a seat. It will just be a few minutes while I talk to the doctor," expounded Nick. Caya refused to sit. "I will come with you." Nick was use to giving orders and having them obeyed; therefore, it came as a great surprise when this woman contradicted his orders. Once he recovered from the surprise he responded, "Caya you need to let me find out the results so I can explain them to you." Not backing down from this man, Caya added, "Nick, I am not an imbecile! I am sure I am capable of understanding whatever the good doctor has to say." "Oh babe, I have no doubt under normal circumstances you are correct, but we are talking about you being a paranormal being. I think I am more than qualified to break this down for you so that you understand."

The anger rose in Caya before she even realized what was happening. She felt the shaking start, followed by the headache. Her skin felt like a fiery furnace and her body was reacting not only by turning her arms furry, but she completely changed as shudders and pain that she had never experienced racked her body as she fell on all fours and started running about the building. "Oh crap!" yelled Nick. He immediately changed to his wolf form and caught her before she escaped the building. He spoke to her wolf through their animal link. He felt her wolf calming. It was very excited to be released. Nick had to use his Alpha talents to force the wolf to return power to Caya's human form. The only problem was that Caya didn't know how to change back to her human form.

Through their mind speak, Nick told Caya to focus on her human body. She was to try to think her human form back into existence. Nick knew Caya needed to get back to her human form, but he loved staring at her wolf. She was a chocolate brown with blue eyes. He could have sworn her eyes were green earlier when they stared at each other by the river. Now, they were blue. *How is that possible? Both shades are beautiful on her. Quit ogling your mate idiot. You have to diffuse this situation before someone gets hurt and then Caya feels guilty about it.* Nick tried again to appeal to Caya to return to her human form.

Caya could feel Nick's thoughts. *How can I feel thoughts? I am such a novice at this. How am I supposed to return to me? I am not sure I want to go through that again. When I changed, it was like every bone in my body was breaking and forming a new body. The pain was excruciating. I am in no hurry to repeat that feeling. Could someone die from excessive pain? I* ***was*** *dying when I changed. I was no longer* ***me****. I was a beast! Ok. I need to think of myself in human form and will my body to return to that form. What does he think I am a magician? Oh, sure. I will just pull a human body out of my hat. I do want to be me again, minus the pain. I don't want to be an animal. I just want to be Caya Braswell, lowly school teacher, nothing exciting about that. I don't want to be a ferocious wolf, even if I have never felt stronger or faster in this body. Come on Caya get back to reality, get back to* ***you****.*

Caya felt her body shudder once again. There was no headache this time, but the pain came like a punch in the gut. Once the shuddering and pain stopped, she looked up to find Nick standing over her in his human body. "Well, that didn't go as planned," smirked Nick. "Caya, please understand. I am not insulting your intelligence. I just think that I can explain things about this way of life to you and what is going on with your body better than Dr. Hill. Will you wait while I talk to him without getting angry and forcing another change?" *Well I had to give it to him. He seemed sincere about his intentions.* "Ok, but can we make it quick. This wolf stuff is making me hungry," replied Caya. Caya always became hungry when she was worried. She could down a whole bag of Lindt chocolates in one sitting if she allowed herself. This was no time to be thinking of food, but she couldn't ignore the gnawing in her stomach.

Chapter 3

Caya couldn't help fidgeting. While Nick spoke to the good doctor, Caya was kneading her hands, and then she would get up and pace the hallway. She would see Nick glance at her and she would sit again. After a few, short minutes she would be up again repeating the routine. Nick came out of the doctor's office and his brow was furrowed, his jaw had tightened, and if steam could come out of his ears it would be an eruption. Caya jumped up. "Well, what did Dr. Jekyll; I mean Hill, have to say? Am I a normal werewolf specimen or are there too many abnormalities and I only have a few months to live?" Nick looked down at Caya with softening eyes and said, "Why don't we discuss this over dinner. You said you were starving." Caya was thinking that the change in his visage suggested the latter medical deduction. Nick put his hand at her back and guided her out of the medical facility and to his truck. Even with running boards he felt it necessary to help her into the vehicle. As he lifted himself in the driver's seat, Caya faced him. She could hear the breaking of her voice as she asked, "WW-here are we headed now." Nick started the truck and let it idle for a minute before responding. "We are going to my house. My mom cooks for me." Nick did not miss Caya's reaction to his statement, the lifted, right eyebrow, the way her lips formed an O as she replied, "You still live with your mother?" Nick couldn't help but burst out in laughter. "Well you could say that she lives with me." The truck pulled away from the medical building and Caya couldn't help but notice Dr. Hill staring at them from his office window. Even the good doctor had worry lines across his graying brow.

The asphalt road turned into gravel as they drove the short distance to Nick's humble abode. Yeah right, it was anything but humble. They pulled up to a log cabin that looked as if it amassed four acres. The landscaping resembled a painter's pallet with the multitude of colors that surrounded the home. The logs looked to be new and the roof was laden with forest green metal. The shutters along the windows were the color of the roof. If cabins could be mansions, this one was the mansion of all mansions, climbing three stories. Caya forgot about her medical situation for the moment as she took in this monstrosity of a home. "Does the whole pack live here?" Nick turned the truck off and eased out to help her from the truck. "No. Those who have started their own families have built homes on our estate. Some of my single friends, my mom and now you live here with me." *Ewe that sounds very permanent,* thought Caya. *Do I want to live here with him? I would prefer just a short vacation to learn the way of werewolves, wouldn't I?* Nick recognized her reluctance to go in the house. "We better get a move on or mom will be after us about letting the food get cold."

As Nick opened the wooden, green door Caya turned toward the truck to see Mt. Rainier as a backdrop from the wrap-around front porch. "Beautiful," was all Caya managed to say. With a view like this, why shouldn't she stay for a while, at least until she understood where her new life might lead her. Nick replied, "I think this view is the most picturesque in this part of the country." After they took in the view for a few minutes, Caya turned back to Nick. Nick held his hand up to her for a brief moment as if to halt her progress. "My mom has just been informed about my finding my mate. She may be very enthusiastic as she has been waiting for this day for some twenty-eight years. She is going to want to hug you, feed you, and more than likely put you through the inquisition. When you have had all you can take, just mention that I am going to show you the lake and we better go before sundown. I will know from that remark that I need to rescue you." Caya wanted to discuss what happened at the doctor's office and this was only going to delay that conversation. *I guess that it will be better to meet his mother before he becomes the bearer of bad news.* Caya just gave a little nod in Nick's direction as he ushered her into the living area of the cabin. Caya didn't realize she was so exhausted until she took in the plush, brown couch that took up a large portion of the room. Then, she spotted the plush, reclining rocker that matched the sectional, what she wouldn't give to lower herself in that rocker and rock all of her worry and apprehension away. You would think with a sixty inch flat screen in here the whole pack would be camped out in here. Caya's stomach grumblings brought her out of her house inspection mode. Voices could be heard coming from the next room. Nick led her into the kitchen that was down a short hallway to the right of the living room, *how convenient for hungry, male werewolves*, thought Caya.

Upon entering the kitchen, Caya noticed the large, wooden table that appeared to house twenty chairs. Caya couldn't believe what she was seeing. A huge kitchen with contemporary cabinets, appliances, and quartz countertops filled the room. A woman all of Caya's stature of 5'6" rushed over to them. She had auburn hair with some graying roots that defined her need to wear them with honor for a life that had not always been easy. As Nick had predicted, she wrapped her arms around Caya and flamboyantly said, "Oh you are finally here. I hope you like grilled salmon. The boys caught it earlier and I told them I would cook it for dinner. I am Halina Wilhelm and we are so glad that you are here. Please sit and start eating." Caya was embarrassed as her stomach continued to rumble so everyone from here to Tacoma could hear it. Caya stated, "I love salmon. Thank you for preparing my dinner. It smells delicious." Nick grinned as he pulled a chair out for Caya. Apparently, she had gained brownie points with her remarks to his mother. Another young woman, with the same brown hair with auburn highlights that adorned Nick's head, entered the room. She was very shy as she didn't look Caya in the eye. She appeared to be about Nick's age. Halina said, "Felicia will you help me put the rest of this food on the table? It will just be the four of us tonight. The guys are out running off their extra energy." Nick interrupted, "Caya this is my younger sister Felicia. Felicia this is Caya Braswell." Without meeting Caya's gaze, Felicia replied, "Nice to meet you Caya. I hope you are happy here. I have placed some clothing in your room. We appear to be the about the same size." Caya looked perplexed as she met Nick's eyes. Nick interjected, "We will go to your home and get what you need tomorrow." Caya corrected him by saying, "My apartment. My friend since middle school and I live together. She will be worried about me. I will call her after dinner. "Thank you for being so kind as to loan me some of your clothing. I will wash and return it as soon as I have my own clothes with me." Felicia finally met Caya's gaze and replied, "Don't worry about it. I am more than happy to help." With this one interaction, Caya could tell that she and Felicia could be good friends. Perhaps she would be some comfort as Caya became associated with her new identity. At that thought, Caya felt panic as she worried that she would never be herself again. Coming out of her reverie, Caya realized Nick was correct when he assumed his mother would rival the Spanish Inquisition. She had to know Caya's age, where and what she taught, and the grade level. She was surprised to learn that Caya taught eleventh grade English at Stadium High School in Tacoma. Many people assumed that she couldn't hold her own with high school students, but Caya was a force to be reckoned with and she had very few problems with the hormonal adolescents. When Caya related the car accident that had taken the lives of her parents, she saw such empathy in Halina's face. The older woman wanted to know how Caya and Nick met and to that Nick responded, "Mom don't quill her all night. I promised to show her the lake before sundown. Caya, if you have had your fill we should go see the lake." Caya insisted, "I should help your mother clean up since she was so kind to cook for me." Halina started clearing the table declaring, "No, you two go ahead. There is not much daylight left. Felicia and I will have this taken care of in no time at all. Go, get out of here." She gave each a hug and pushed them out the kitchen door. As they walked out the door, Caya punched Nick lightly in the stomach and said, "I didn't hint that I needed a rescue." Nick raised an eyebrow in all seriousness and acknowledged, "I am the one that needed the rescue. I did not want to relate how I happened upon you and your boyfriend and then kidnapped you and forced you to see the doctor. I don't think that is the romantic story she was eagerly awaiting." Caya did not miss the strain in his voice as he said, "your boyfriend." Caya glided down the steps and said, "No, I guess not."

They walked a half mile through the woods before Caya stopped mid-step, turned and found her face implanted in Nick's bulging chest. He stopped abruptly and rested his hands on her shoulders to keep them both from toppling onto the forest floor. "Are you going to tell me what Dr. Hill said? I am really getting tired of these delay tactics." Nick was at a loss of how to explain to this young woman what he had learned from the doctor. "Caya I am not trying to delay the inevitable. I know you want to know, but out of consideration for you I did not want to discuss this in front of my family. I thought if I took you to the lake that it might have a calming effect on you." Caya stared into those emerald orbs and saw a softness that she had not seen there since they had become acquainted. She swallowed and looked over his shoulder and asked, "How much further?" He wasn't having it. He tilted his head so that she was looking into those gems again and replied, "Not much further." He turned her around and they headed deeper into the woods. They did not try to take quiet steps and squirrels and rabbits were scampering out of their way. Caya could see an opening up ahead in the woods and as she drew closer it was like she could smell the lake. They found a rock formation at the edge of the lake and settled themselves there. The slight breeze around the lake blew a few hairs into Caya's face. As she moved to put the hair behind her ear, Nick spoke. "This is my favorite place. This is where I come to get away and think." Caya let this revelation sink in as she realized he had brought her here to his favorite place.

"Caya I need you to look at me and try to stay calm as I relate to you what Dr. Hill has discovered about you." Caya was already getting panic stricken. She was afraid that she would change again. She didn't want to, but she didn't know how to stop it. Just knowing it could happen anytime put her in a state of apprehension. Nick continued, "Well, you definitely have werewolf blood in your veins. The question is why have you waited until what, twenty years to change? Most werewolves change by their third year." Caya responded with, "Twenty-five." With head lowered she said, "I am abnormal, as if being a werewolf is not abnormal enough, now I find out I am an abnormal werewolf." Nick lifted her chin toward him as he said, "Caya you are not abnormal. You are beautiful and smart. Once you become accustomed to this way of life, you will never want to go back to the way you were." Caya jumped to her feet and faced the lake as she spouted, "Never! There is no way I will ever want to become an animal! I just want to be me!" Nick joined her by the lake. "You will still be you, but you will have the ability to change forms at will. You will be strong, fast, and have keen senses." He didn't touch her. He continued to face the lake and gave her a few minutes to reflect on what he had said. She was drawn from her reverie when he spoke, "Caya did someone bite you?" Caya turned toward Nick with disbelief in her eyes. Caya responded, "What? I think Jamey Osborne did when we were in daycare at age two. You know those terrible twos resemble animalistic behavior." Nick's mouth twitched despite his seriousness. "Caya, I love how you use humor as a coping mechanism, but I really need you to think. You would have had to be bitten or have a blood transfusion from another werewolf. It is obvious that you were not born with werewolf blood." Caya could not fathom what Nick was insinuating. No one had bitten her. She looked at the scar running from her shoulder to her elbow. She hoped with more time the scar would become less noticeable. She couldn't remember all of the details of the accident. The last thing she remembered was sliding down the rocky cliff. She had to talk to Rayna and James. *Is it possible that James could have infected me? That would mean, oh no!*

Chapter 4

Caya paced along the water's edge consumed with her thoughts. *How can someone date another person for four months and not know he is a werewolf? It is true that you don't really know someone until you live with him.* She also remembered James talking to Nick by the river as if they knew each other and they were discussing territory. She remembered his stating that all of the males around her, at that time, were werewolves. *He **is** a werewolf.* She did not want to believe it. Nick was growing more concerned the longer she paced. He would be staring at those long legs if he was not so consumed with watching the different contortions that her face was making as she was pacing. He allowed himself to believe that the longer she paced without changing, the better her emotional stability. He didn't need her to change and go on a furious rampage through the estate. Word of Nick having found his mate had spread among the pack, but not everyone had met her and he didn't want one of his pack responsible for any harm that may come to an out-of-control werewolf on his property.

Caya stopped abruptly. She turned to look at Nick and tears started rolling down her cheeks. "How could he do this to me?" Nick jumped off his rocky seat and wrapped his well-toned arms around her. "So you know who did this to you? Do you remember someone biting you or have you had a blood transfusion recently?" Caya rested her head on Nick's shoulder. She could smell his body wash, something with a hint of musk. That smell would forever be engrained into her senses. She was able to quit crying long enough to answer him. "A few weeks ago I had an accident." She removed her arms from around his waist and stared at her scar. Nick had noticed the scar earlier, but he didn't realize that it was new. Apparently, her new wolf anatomy was healing it, but not at the speed an established werewolf would heal. "I don't remember much about the accident. I guess I could have had a transfusion. Several of us were out hiking and it started raining and I slid off a cliff. I don't remember anything beyond sliding down a huge rock. He said he loved me. How could he turn me into this animal! I have to talk to James. I have to find out what has happened to me." The crying was punctuated by fury as she stomped off toward the house. Nick caught up with her and grabbed her arm and twirled her around so that she was facing him. "Are you saying that you think James is responsible for your werewolf tendencies?" Caya continued to cry and stammered, "I don't know wha-what to think." Nick let her cry for another minute and then she pulled away from him and started toward the house again. Nick was thankful that through all of this emotion that she did not change. They walked back to the cabin without another word between them. As they rounded the house, Nick could feel the change in his mate's emotion. He could feel her changing from sad and confused to furious. "Caya wait! Don't go inside just yet. Talk to me." Caya turned on her heel and about plowed over him. He steadied her by the shoulders once again. Caya peered down at her hands and she could see the fur engulfing her hands. "Oh no, not again!" Nick held her so she couldn't run from him. He soothingly replied, "It is ok. I am right here. Let the change happen. Your wolf needs to protect you right now." "I don't want to change!" screamed Caya. Patiently, Nick continued to speak softly, reassuring her. "It is normal for you to be afraid. This is all new to you. I promise the more you change the easier it will get. It will not hurt as bad once you have allowed the changing to become part of your daily routine." Caya's eyes were wide and angry as she screamed and changed to her animal body. Nick remained calm and stayed in human form. He could still speak to her in this form, but hearing thoughts were not as clear as when in wolf form. He tried to keep his hand on her back and rub her to help soothe her, but before he could comfort her, she ran back into the woods.

Nick let the change overcome him and he chased after his mate. In this form, he could feel her pain stabbing at his heart. He allowed her to run until her wolf was consoled. He would just keep track of her; keep her from hurting herself or anyone else. When she was ready, she would come to him and he would help coax her back to her human form. It troubled Nick immensely that his mate hated her wolf form. Nick knew if she would embrace it that Caya would love being a werewolf just as much as she loved being human. How could he be with her if she hated the werewolf way of life? He was thankful that he had found Caya, but he was enraged that her supposed boyfriend could have changed her without her consent. He had to get his anger under control before she picked up on it. He needed to remain calm so that he could help calm her. Running was helping calm them both. She should be exhausted with all of the excitement and then all of the running they had participated in today.

Nick was correct. After her wolf had taken over and was in control of her emotions, she was stalking back towards him. He couldn't get over that beautiful coat of fur on her. Even angry, he loved this wolf that was standing before him. Now, the plan was to get **her** to see that beauty. Nick spoke to her through her thoughts. He reminded her to think of changing back into her human form. It did take a while for her to change back to a human, but with each try it would become easier for her, eventually she would not mind the change at all. It would become natural to her.

His mate was so exhausted that once she changed she fell in a pile of thick grass and he picked her up and carried her to the house. Once inside, he took her to a room off the living room. He carried her easily in his arms and opened the door to a room draped with beautiful lavender curtains and the smell of spring flowers. The bedspread was white with lilacs floating across it. He placed her on the bed so gently that she couldn't help but wonder if he was always this gentle. "You have had a long day. You should shower and go to bed for the night. I will see you at breakfast in the morning. We don't have to sort this all out tonight. Our brains need rest before they become overloaded. If you need anything my room is upstairs, the first room on the left. Felicia's room is two doors down from your room. He looked at her with pleading eyes as he backed away toward the door. She could see compassion, remorse, longing, and maybe even fear in those emerald gems. Unfortunately, all she could think about at the moment was what would tomorrow hold?

Caya awoke with a start. She had no idea where she was. This was definitely not her room. As she took in the lavender décor of the room, she remembered the events of last night and Nick placing her in bed in this room. The memories of last night kept bombarding her and she decided she needed to dress and get answers. After she dressed, she headed to the kitchen where she could clearly hear every word of what was being said even from her bedroom door. *How is this possible? Oh yeah, werewolf senses. This might come in handy.* She stopped just outside the kitchen and listened to Nick who was apparently talking to his bestie, Seth. Seth asked, "How many men do we need for this move?" Nick replied, "I am not sure. I haven't been to her apartment." Caya remembered they were supposed to go to her apartment to pick up her belongings this morning. *I really need to speak to James, but how will I convince Nick that this is a priority. I have a feeling that he will not let me anywhere near James.* The aroma of the cooked bacon brought Caya into the kitchen. Everyone looked at her as she entered. Nick stood and walked over and pulled her chair out for her. "What took you so long to come in here to eat?" questioned Nick. Caya's face turned beet red. She had forgotten that if she had heightened senses now so did Nick and he was far more accustomed to embracing his ability. He probably heard her get out of bed so of course he would know that she stood outside the kitchen. Caya responded that she was just making sure she was presentable upon entering. Nick raised his right eyebrow in response. Boy was that sexy. Halina placed a plate with a variety of breakfast items in front of her. Her eyes became as big as saucers. Nick commented on how his mom was use to preparing for hungry, male wolves.

After Caya felt she would explode from her glutinous meal, Nick asked her how many truckloads it would take to move her stuff to the estate. Caya was not sure of the answer. Caya asked, "Are we talking pickup trucks or moving trucks?" Nick asked, "Can we use pickups or do you have so much we need moving trucks?" Caya's hurt expression did not escape him. "I have no idea how much we will be moving and I have never seen your apartment. I didn't mean to offend you," Nick backpedaled. "I would think maybe four pickup truck loads would get it all. I can always bring my clothes in my car. Nick looked at Seth and Seth nodded. Seth left and Nick rose from his chair and pulled Caya's chair out for her. As she stood she couldn't help but feel the raw energy coming from Nick. Her face started coloring once again. Intent on distracting her thoughts, she told him that she needed to call Rayna and let her know that she was safe and would be coming to the apartment shortly.

While Caya was making her call, Nick made a few calls of his own. He needed to take care of some business before he spent the day playing mover. Rayna answered the phone on the first ring. Breathlessly, she answered, "Girlfriend where are you? I have been going out of my mind. Lars said you met someone and left to catch up with your friend. This is so not like you and James was clearly frustrated and went straight home when we left the river. I was so worried. Are you on your way home? Do I need to come get you or call James?" Caya realized she would never get a chance to talk unless she just hijacked the conversation, the one-sided conversation.

"Rayna I am fine. I am coming home and please do not call James. I need to talk to you, but I know you have to work. This is really important and I don't want to discuss it over the phone. Could you wait for me? I will be there soon." There was a long silence over the line before Rayna replied. "I will wait, but I know there is something terribly wrong with you. You don't act like this. I can't wait to hear what you have to say." "Thanks Rayna and I will be there as soon as I can." Nick had stepped into the living room to make his calls and he walked back into the kitchen as Caya was pressing the end button on her phone. "Are you ready?" asked Nick. "No, but I don't have a choice," sulked Caya. Caya had no idea how she was going to explain to Rayna that she was moving out and moving in with a man that she just met a few hours ago.

After Nick helped Caya into the truck, three other trucks pulled in behind him. Caya could see that Seth was in the truck directly behind Nick's truck. Nick was conversing with Seth and Nick returned to the truck and slid in behind the wheel. As they pulled out of the circular drive, Nick told Caya she would need to give him her address so he could enter it into his GPS. After Nick had the address programmed into the GPS, he called Seth and gave him the address. Caya said, "You know you are supposed to be programming that thing before we start moving. You even have to agree to the onscreen prompt that you will not operate it while moving." Nick kept his eyes on the road as he replied, "Yes mother. I will keep that in mind when you are with me in the future, but I think we are safe as we are still on the drive into the estate which happens to be private, with little traffic." Caya crossed her arms across her chest. "Furthermore, you need to put your seatbelt on since we are practicing driving safety," admonished Nick. Caya glared at him as she buckled her seatbelt and she didn't miss the lift of one side of his mouth as he was trying not to laugh.

Caya was thankful that they rode in silence the rest of the way to her apartment. She had time to think about what she would say to Rayna. However, she still wasn't sure what to tell her. She had tossed several ideas around in her head, but none of them would satisfy Rayna. Caya decided to stick as close to the truth as she could and let the conversation play out as it may. As they pulled up in front of the apartment, Caya looked over at Nick. He had turned the truck off and was staring at the apartment complex in front of him. He calmly asked, "What are you going to tell her?" Caya was all fumbling hands as she replied, "I don't know. I am going to stick to the truth as best I can." Nick looked at her with concern. "You know you can't tell her about what has happened to you or about my pack without endangering all of us."

Caya looked at him and could see he was really worried about how this was going to play out. Caya placed a hand on his arm and looked into those emerald eyes. She hoped she was reassuring him that she would keep his secret. There was no verbal response from Caya, only the physical. She hoped that he understood and that was enough for him. She released her hold on him, opened the truck door and jumped out. When she looked up at him from the road, she gave him a little wink and a smile and then closed the door. He jumped out and was at her side in one second. She knew that he wouldn't relax until they were back at his house, but she hoped that her last communication put him somewhat at ease. As they walked up to the door, Caya was feeling for her keys in her purse and Nick said, "I see you are exerting your independence already." After finding the key, Caya looked up at him and said, "I like a gentleman to open my door, but sometimes I need to prove that I can take care of myself." "Duly noted ma'am, but this is a conversation for another time." Caya need not have fumbled for her key because as she put it in the lock the door flew open and Rayna pulled her into a hug that just about suffocated her.

Nick could tell that these two were very close and he saw the relief on Rayna's face as she and Caya held each other. He looked down at his feet until they broke apart and then he followed them into the apartment. Caya made the introductions while Rayna just scowled at Nick. Rayna imbued, "What have you done to my sister? She is not acting like herself. I don't think for a minute that you are an old friend with whom she has reunited. I have known her way too long and I have never seen you." Caya knew she had to calm her friend down before she started physically defending her. Caya looked her in the eye and said, "Rayna I know you care about me and I want you to know that I am fine. This is Nick and I have chosen to move in with him and his family. I have never believed in love at first sight, but when we ran into him and his friends at the river I immediately felt the connection between us. I know this is unlike me, but I am telling you that Nick and I have a connection that we wish to explore. Please trust me."

Caya knew this would not be enough to get Rayna off Nick's case, but she had to start somewhere and she was trying her best to stick to the truth and not mislead her. Rayna slid her eyes from Nick to Caya. "What about James? You have dated him for four months and you just see some hot guy and you leave with the hot guy and say adios to your boyfriend. Have you been brainwashed! You are not the friend that I have grown up with and love." Caya disarmed Rayna by saying, "You are right Rayna. I am not me, but I have to explore this new me and that exploration involves Nick."

Rayna was silent for several minutes. Caya looked at Nick and told him where her room was. Nick nodded and went outside to tell the others and create a plan of action. Caya returned her attention to Rayna who was clearly dumbfounded by her roomie's explanation. Caya chose to speak while she could as this silence was an anomaly with Rayna. "Rayna you are my best friend and that will not change. I still love you like a sister. We will still do things together even though we are not living together." Tears rolled down Rayna's cheeks. Caya embraced her and started spilling her own tears. When the men entered, they took one look at them and high-tailed it to Caya's room to begin work. They didn't want any part in this emotional goodbye.

The girls cried for a time and then pulled apart and smiled at each other. "You better not forget me," demanded Rayna. "No way, you are my sister," declared Caya. Knowing Nick could hear even upstairs, she added, "and there is no way that Nick can replace that." "Nor would I want to," replied Nick through their mental connection. *What in the world!* Emotions must make that connection stronger because Caya was amazed at how clearly she heard Nick's thoughts from upstairs.

They had loaded all of Caya's furniture and were carrying the last load of boxes to the truck. One of the guys was complaining about the number of books Caya had that needed to be moved. Nick just patted him on the shoulder and reminded him that she could have her own house full of stuff to move. The young werewolf just shook his head as he headed out the door and to the truck with the box. Nick turned to Rayna and said, "Rayna I know you feel as though I am coming in between you and your best friend. I want you to know that I will not keep Caya from seeing you. I know that you two have your own connection and because of that I hope that one day you will respect the connection that she and I share. I promise to take care of her. Also, I want you to know that I will pay her rent until you find another roommate. I don't want to cause you a financial hardship on top of the emotional one that I have already caused." Rayna held Nick's gaze while Caya held hope that one day these two would be friends.

Rayna expounded, "Nick I do not know you, but I hope you are being sincere. I want you to rest assured that if you hurt her physically or emotionally you will answer to me. Are we clear?" Nick assented and went to help with the rest of the boxes. The ladies said their tearful goodbyes with Caya promising to call and get together with Rayna soon. As Rayna walked Caya to the truck, Caya noticed the serious visage on Nick and Seth. Nick turned to Caya and said, "Caya, we need to go, if you have said your goodbyes." Caya wasn't sure what was happening, but she could tell he was in a hurry so she allowed him to open her door and help her in the truck. Nick turned to Rayna. "It was nice to meet you and I look forward to seeing you soon Rayna." "Oh don't worry. I will be keeping tabs on Caya and you will see me soon and often Nick," Rayna said matter-of-factly.

As they pulled away from the apartment complex, Caya noticed the reason for Nick's hasty retreat. Down a side road, Caya spotted James' truck. She just hoped James didn't try to follow them and start a fight. She was disappointed that she wouldn't be able to interrogate him about how she had become a werewolf. As Nick would say, "That is a conversation for another time." Caya knew she wouldn't be able to hold out on that conversation for much longer. James had a lot of explaining to do.

Chapter 5

As the convoy approached the house, Caya came out of her daydream. She had been contemplating how her meeting with James would go, whenever it finally happened. She allowed the image of her tearing him to shreds before he could get a word out of his treacherous mouth to enter her mind. However, she soon realized that wouldn't work because she would never get her answers. *Why am I having these violent tendencies? I am not a violent person. Oh yes, I am an animal. I am sure this is just my animal instinct kicking in.*

Before she could get any further immersed into her daydream, Nick was helping her out of the truck once again. Nick stepped over to Seth's truck and told him to take the boxes of books to the empty room on the third floor with the balcony. He told Aaron and the other guys to help Seth. Caya could tell that the men were used to taking orders from Nick and Nick was very comfortable giving them. He led Caya to the house and as they entered he asked where she would like her clothes and other personal belongings placed in the room. Upon entering the bedroom, she looked around and couldn't quite get the feel of how to set it up. She just told Nick to have them put the boxes on the floor around the room and throw the clothes that were on hangers on her bed. She wouldn't be working; therefore, she would have plenty of time to arrange her things. Once he was satisfied with the placement of her belongings, Nick left to give more orders.

Caya looked around again trying to get in her mind where to start. Before she knew it, the guys were bringing her prized possessions in and placing them in her room. At one point, she stepped outside her room and saw the men carrying her boxes of books upstairs. Although the men carried the boxes as if they were as light as a feather, she felt guilty for having so many books. However, if she had to move, her books were coming with her. She took a break from her unpacking to go upstairs to see where the rest of her belongings would reside. As she walked up the stairs, she could see the wonderful workmanship that went into the building of the staircase. The railing had pictures of wolves carved into the wood. The wood had been sanded to a smooth, glossy texture. Trees surrounded each wolf scene. As she admired the craftsmanship, Nick appeared at the top of the stairs. "I thought I heard you." Caya tore her attention from the railing and asked, "Who made this?" Nick followed her gaze to the wolf scenes on the staircase. "Will and his dad do woodwork. I love all of the detail they put into their work." Caya looked into his eyes and said, "It is beautiful." Nick responded with, "I agree." He turned to go up to the next flight of stairs. "Were you coming up to see where we were storing your books?" "Yes, and I wanted to admire the rest of your mansion." Nick turned so red that Caya couldn't help but chuckle at his reaction. "You need a big house for a big family," he admonished.

As they topped the staircase, Nick rounded on Caya and almost made her lose her balance. He quickly grabbed her arm and pulled her to him. "Sorry, I didn't mean to scare you. I was just going to ask you a question." After regaining her balance, she was keenly aware that her face was planted into Nick's hard chest. She could hear his heartbeat beating rapidly inside. Her eyes slowly traveled from his chest to his eyes. She could see concern dancing in those emerald orbs, and frown lines between them. "Wh-at did you want to ask?" Once again Nick's face and neck took on a rosy tint. "I want to do something special for you, but I am afraid you will take my offer the wrong way." Caya's eyes grew as she could not imagine what he meant by this statement. Nick continued, "I want to have Will's dad make you some new bookcases for your books. There is nothing wrong with your bookcases, but I thought we could have built-in bookshelves and that would give you more room for your books. You could have the whole room as your library. You could decorate it however you would like."

His eyes traveled to his boots. Caya was dumbfounded. In just a matter of hours of knowing her, he had decided to create something special for her. He must know how much her books mean to her and he wants to create a unique home for them. That this stranger would latch on to such a personal part of her overwhelmed Caya. She didn't know what to say to him. Before she realized what she was doing, she had grabbed his shoulders and was pulling him to her. The hug lasted for several minutes. She was determined not to cry even though she could feel the pin pricks at the back of her eyes.

Nick stood there holding her until she broke the embrace, at which time he led her to her library. The guys were carefully arranging the boxes in the center of the floor, but leaving a walkway through them. Caya had no doubt that this too was a directive from Nick. Caya noticed how well organized the guys had kept her books. The boxes had alphabetical labeling on them. She was taken aback that they would have arranged these books in such a manner. Most men would have just thrown them in a box and made quick work of the job. She had a lot to learn about Nick and to her consternation she decided she was going to enjoy every minute of it.

After dinner, Caya went back to her bedroom to hang the rest of her clothes in the closet. After all, she would need to clear her bed in order to sleep tonight. She was surprised how quickly the guys unloaded the trucks. They had asked if she needed help unpacking, but she assured them that she needed to take her time to decide what do with everything and they needn't wait on her to make those decisions. She couldn't help but notice how grateful they appeared at that news.

As she was beginning to tire from the day, her thoughts drifted back to James. She still felt the betrayal run through her body as if she had a cold chill about her. He had changed her life forever and not in a good way. She would never be herself again. She suddenly felt terrified at the prospect of being a werewolf. She was confused and scared a little before, but now it was really dawning on her that she was a wolf being constrained by her human form. She was having trouble breathing. She needed to get some air. She left her room and ran up the stairs to the top floor. She ran through the library and onto the balcony. As she pushed the french doors open, she was accosted by the most beautiful sunset she had ever seen. The serene, picturesque view calmed her so that her breathing returned to normal. As her eyes scanned the world beneath her, she spotted the most majestic, brown wolf at the edge of the woods. His green eyes peered through to her soul before he turned and ran into the forest. Minutes later, Caya heard the howl of that same wolf in the distance. She didn't know how she knew that it was the same wolf, but deep down she knew his voice already.

Chapter 6

The next morning at breakfast, Caya was putting her dishes in the dishwasher and looked out the window to find James' truck pulling into the driveway. Anger welled up inside her. She ran out of the kitchen, out the front door, down the stairs into Seth's massive chest. She could no longer see James, but she heard him yell, "Let her go! I'm not going to hurt her." Seth replied, "It's not you I am worried about. I am protecting you from one disgruntled, new werewolf who wants to send you into the next world." Caya noticed the smile on Seth's face as he looked down at her. Nick was making his way down the steps to them as he said, "Seth let her go. They have business to resolve." Seth raised an eyebrow to Nick, questioning his judgement, but let Caya resume her determined gait toward James.

Caya, not trusting herself to get any closer, stopped about ten yards from her former boyfriend. James could see that her eyes were blazing and he was wondering how long it would be before she started to change. Caya, not waiting a minute longer, commenced the questioning. "James, what did you do to me!?" James looked straight into her eyes and then down at his worn boots. "Caya, you deserve to know the truth, but you need to come with me so that I may explain this without an audience." Nick stepped just behind her and replied, "Whatever you have to say to her can be said right here and right now. I don't think it is the audience you should be focused on." James looked at Nick with disdain.

He looked from Nick to her and his visage softened. "Caya, how much of the accident on the cliff do you remember?" Caya gathered herself long enough to reply, "I do not remember anything but sliding toward the edge of the cliff." James supplied his version of the rest of the story. "Well, you did slide off the cliff and landed on a ledge about fifteen feet below. As you were trying to grab something to break your fall, your arm was cut by a jagged tree stump. Lars and I had to change to get to you quick because you were bleeding profusely. You were unresponsive, but still breathing. Lars' medical training allowed him to recognize that you were going into shock. We had to return to our human forms to actually carry you back up to the top of the cliff. We tied off your arm just above the cut with my shirt, but you were bleeding through the shirt." James paused and Caya said, "Continue." "By the time we reached the truck we had to make a tourniquet to staunch the bleeding. Lars suggested that we return to our pack doctor as it was closer than the hospital and we were running out of time."

Looking for understanding, James continued, "Caya, you could have died. We were doing what we thought best at the time. When we arrived, our doctor removed the tourniquet and had to repair a severed artery. Once he performed surgery, you needed a blood transfusion and we did not have pure human blood on hand. I made the decision to give you some of my blood." Looking at his feet once again, James continued. "We did not know how you would react to my werewolf blood, but we knew there was no time to get you to the hospital and even if we did we would have had to move you and that may have caused more damage." Tears welled up in James' eyes as he looked at her. "I had to do something! I couldn't sit there and watch the life being sucked out of you!" "I made the decisions I made because I love you. I hope one day you will forgive me."

Caya stood as still as a statue. Her breathing became erratic as she said in her too calm voice, "You had no right to make the decision to turn me into this animal. I would rather be dead." As she said this her arms became wrapped in fur. She took two steps toward the woods and had completely changed as she descended deep into the forest. Nick stepped toward James and all of the onlookers stiffened. Nick looked James square in the eye and said, "Thank you for saving her life. I can never repay that debt. However, she is right. You had no right to make that decision for her." Nick ran toward the woods and changed in mid-run after reaching the wooded sanctuary.

James gathered is entourage and left the Puyallup reserve. Seth and Aaron returned to the house to get breakfast. Nick kept his distance from his mate. He knew she needed time to run and calm herself. Her wolf needed to protect her. He would just keep an eye on her and he knew she would come to him when she was ready. After running probably 20 miles around the estate, Caya came toward Nick who was still in wolf form. She approached cautiously and Nick could sense her exhaustion. Caya needed no help to change back to her human form this time, but the pain and energy it took showed all over her face. After the change, she collapsed in a pile of leaves on the forest floor. Nick changed to his human form before picking her up in his arms and running back to the house.

He knew she was too exhausted to talk, nor did she probably want to talk about what happened. He just held her close and tried to comfort her as best he could. He wasn't sure that he was giving her what she needed, but he would not leave her side tonight. As they entered the house, he walked over to the couch in the living room and placed her body gently on it. He grabbed a big, fleece throw from the back of the couch and lay down beside her and covered them. He watched her sleep and wondered how fitfully she would sleep this night. Surprisingly, after watching Caya sleep for a while, Nick fell into his own slumber.

Caya awoke the next morning to the sun beaming in from the large window at the head of the couch. She felt restrained and stiff. She realized the reason for the restraint rather quickly.

She could feel heavy limbs encircling her body. Warm breath was blanketing her face. She turned her head slightly to see Nick fast asleep beside her. She couldn't believe that this man was showing her such compassion. He should be running for the hills. She had not been the most stable person in the last few days. He really had to care for her to take care of her like this. As she realized that he was doing just that, tears escaped her eyes and rolled down her cheeks. How could he care for her in this state when he barely even knew her?

Nick awakened to something wet on his arm. He opened his eyes and looked directly into Caya's eyes. She was crying. He wiped a tear from her cheek. He wasn't sure what to say to her. He had been around his sister and mom enough to know that when something was bothering them it was best not to question them. It was a much better idea to wait for them to be forthcoming. He said, "Good morning, sunshine." His smile was like healing powders to a deep cut. She smiled and replied, "Good morning to you and your growling stomach." They both laughed. Nick was quick to add, "I guess breakfast is next on the agenda." They decided to shower and dress for the day before having breakfast.

Nick waited outside her bedroom and when she walked out he turned to go toward the kitchen. Caya grabbed his arm. "Nick, I want to thank you for taking care of me last night." Nick looked into her hazel eyes and replied, "That was the easy part. I will always take care of you Caya. The hard part was not dismembering that traitorous ex-boyfriend of yours." Caya did detect the emphasis on "ex-boyfriend." Nick continued, "Caya I have to say that I am thankful that he saved your life, even if the result was not what you wanted. Without his decision, you would most likely be dead, and without the wolf blood I may have never found my mate. To that end, I owe him my gratitude. However, I agree that he had no right to make the decision that forced you into a werewolf. It infuriates me that he and that quack doctor had no idea what the outcome of that transfusion would be and yet they did it anyway. As far as I know, you are an enigma when it comes to a case like this. We will have to let Dr. Hill keep tabs on you as no one knows how this will affect your health on a long-term basis."

Caya noticed a shadow fall across his visage just before he said, "I don't want you to think that death would be preferable to being a werewolf." Caya continued to stare into his emerald eyes. Finally, she replied, "I can see the hurt in your face every time I complain about being an animal. I understand that this is your way of life and you know no different. However, you must understand that this was thrown upon me late in life. I didn't grow up in your world. I am afraid that I am going to have to ask your patience as I come to terms with my situation. In the last few days, you have been faithful to help me embrace this way of life. Even when I fall short of your expectations, you comfort me and lend me your strength. I think that I am learning a little of what being your mate means. If anyone can help me through this transition,

I see that it is you. Therefore, I want to thank you again for helping me last night and thank you for all you will do in the future to comfort and keep me safe."

Nick wrapped his arm around her waist and said, "I am always here for you and I want you to know that you can ask or tell me anything. This relationship is different than most you have had and we are going to have to communicate with one another and be honest with one another as we make this pilgrimage together." Caya smiled, "Why Nick, you sound almost philosophical. Who knew?" Their stomachs growled in unison. Caya laughed and said, "I guess we better fuel up before starting our pilgrimage." At that comment, they headed toward the kitchen each with an arm wrapped around the other's waist.

Chapter 7

For the next few days Nick and Caya spent a lot of time together. They changed into their wolf forms and ran in the woods twice a day. Nick kept telling Caya the more she changed the easier it would become. Caya wasn't buying what he was selling, but she did like the feel of freedom that enveloped her after the change and she started her run. After the night on the couch, Caya had grown closer to Nick. Even though she was getting to know him better and knowing herself better, she was still afraid of losing herself. One morning after their run, Seth was waiting for them on the front porch. Nick immediately sensed trouble and turned to Caya. "Caya, I have some business that may take me a while. I will find you when I am finished." Caya thought this was odd, but she just smiled and walked past them.

Once they were in Nick's office, Seth began to explain to Nick his concern. "Nick, the pack is getting restless. They are concerned about possible threats Caya may pose to them." Nick's brow furrowed as he lashed out, "Threat! What threat Seth! Caya doesn't pose a threat to these people. She is my mate and they should welcome her as such." Seth countered, "I know, but they have heard rumors about how she became a werewolf. You know that she is, as you call her, an enigma. They are not sure about her stability." Nick took a moment to ponder this revelation. "We need to present her, as my mate, to the pack. We will have a cookout and let them get to know her. They will see she is not a threat to them." Seth backed up as he spoke, "Are you sure about that?" Nick stood and Seth spoke quickly, "We don't know how stable she is. This life is new to her. Every time she loses it she changes. Who is to say that she will not go on a killing rampage at some point if something riles her to that point." Nick was clearly angry as his face was turning a few shades of red. Seth stood his ground as Nick pondered what Seth had said. Seth continued, "Don't get me wrong, man. I think Caya is doing great under the circumstances. I can't say that I wouldn't be killing a few people right now if I were in her shoes. However, I see her and talk to her and am getting to know her. Since the rest of the pack do not know her, I can understand why they are worried. They need you to put their fears to rest."

Nick settled back into his chair, but the furrow remained on his brow. "Thanks Seth. You always have my back. That is why you are my second. You help me see things when I don't want to see them. I think the cookout will be the best plan. I will get with mom and see if she can have this ready in a couple of days. Once I have spoken to her, I will let you spread the invitation." Seth relaxed a little. "That sounds like a plan and for the record you handled that information better than I thought you would. Is this girl mellowing you man?" Nick looked Seth straight in the eye as he replied, "Heck no and don't you think for one minute that she has me whipped either." Nick stood and walked over to his long-time friend. As they wrapped their husky arms around each other's neck Nick replied, "Thanks again man for bringing this to my attention." Seth and Nick laughed in unison while remembering the whipped comment. Seth told Nick that he would always have his back.

While Nick was in his meeting, Caya went up to her library. She couldn't believe she had a library. Nick was working with Seth's dad and his brother to have some bookcases made for the library. Seth's dad and his other brother, Will, make a living working with wood. They made furniture for not only Nick's pack, but people around the area. They were even looking to expand and start taking online orders and shipping furniture. Caya found a box of books and opened it. She found one of her favorites, *The Adventures of Huckleberry Finn*. As she eyed the cover, she thought of her own adventure and wondered how it would end. She could learn a few things from ol' Huck. She was going to have to embrace her adventurous side a little more, if she had one. She should probably find the box with *Shiver*. It was at least a werewolf series. Caya could feel Nick's presence. She still felt that was a little creepy. She was getting in tune with her werewolf hearing as well. This only caused her to be frustrated because all of the sounds distracted her. She could hear boots climbing the stairs. She could tell there was more than one set and assumed it was Nick and Seth coming to find her.

She was sitting on the floor, in the corner, emptying a box of books as Nick came into the room. He was hoping to have her library finished soon. Caya looked up and was startled to see Nick with someone other than Seth. Nick introduced the young man as Will, Seth's brother. Caya was struck by his form fitted t-shirt and his dark brown eyes. He appeared to be four or five years younger than Nick and Seth. Will smiled and walked over to her. He put out his hand and told her he was pleased to meet her. Caya smiled and relaxed as soon as he smiled. That smile just made her feel comfortable and at ease.

Will had come to measure and get specifics as to what type of shelves Caya had in mind. He suggested she might want to stick to solid wood and maybe have molding at the top corners that would reflect her personal taste. She was no furniture manufacturer and had no idea what she wanted. Will gave some suggestions, some of which she accepted and some she did not. She finally decided on solid oak with a medium wood stain. They would custom make bookcases to fill every wall, with the exception of one corner where she would have furniture that would give her a comfortable place to read. While they were discussing the specifics of the room, a thought came to her. She abruptly turned to Will and said, "What about books? Can you make the top molding so that it resembles a line of opened books?" Will looked at her in surprise. He replied, "This will be a new one for us, but I think I understand what you have in mind. We can certainly try, but it will take a lot of handcrafting so it will not be cheap." Caya's smile started to turn into a frown, but Nick quickly told Will that price was no object. He should try to tailor the bookcases to Caya's specifications if at all possible. Will left promising to bring a piece of the custom molding for her inspection the next day.

Finally, Caya was beginning to become excited about her new home. After their meeting with Will, Caya started wondering what Nick did for a living that enabled him to live in such a nice home and afford custom furniture. That evening before their run she asked him about his career. Nick was a little taken aback by this question. He replied that he and Seth were in the computer software business. Caya was intrigued by his answer. "What type of software do you create?" Nick replied, "We make security software for the government. I am not at liberty to discuss it further." *Wow, I didn't see that coming,* thought Caya. "Is your office in town," inquired Caya. "You have been to my office several times. My job allows me to work from home."

As they entered the woods, Caya could smell the approaching rain. All of her senses were becoming heightened which unnerved her. One thing about being a wolf in the rain is that you didn't have to worry about your hair. She and Nick ran toward their lake as thunder started to rumble in the distance.

Once they were home, Nick asked his mom about the cookout. Halina told Nick that she would be able to have everything ready in a couple of days. The cookout was news to Caya. Nick explained that he wanted the pack to meet her so they would feel more comfortable around her. Caya's response was unexpected. "You are inviting the whole pack?" Nick replied, "Well, as many as can make it. From what I gather, everyone is intrigued by you so I am guessing there will be quite the turnout." Halina walked over to Caya and put an arm around her. "Honey, everyone will love you just like we do. If you are going to be mated with an Alpha, you are going to have to get used to being on display." *On display? I am not some Holiday Barbie to be placed on a shelf for visitors to admire.* Nick walked over to her and placed his large, strong hands on her shoulders. He looked her straight in the eye and said, "They will love you. You will not be alone. Just be you." *Just be me. I don't even know who that is anymore.*

Two days later, the cookout was underway. Halina was ordering everyone around the kitchen. The men were grilling and everyone was hoping the cookout would be over before those big, gray clouds decided to douse everyone like a sprinkler. There was a stage in the center of what appeared to be the pack meeting field. While Nick and Seth grilled dinner, Aaron and Will were setting up the stage and an audio system. Once the hamburgers and hotdogs were cooked and the side items and condiments were arranged on long buffet tables outside, everyone started mulling around and fixing their plates. Caya couldn't help but notice everyone looking her way. Even the children eyed her as they passed. She was feeling very uncomfortable. Nick tried to cajole her to eat, but her stomach was doing summersaults and eating was the last thing she wanted to do.

Once people finished their meal, they started creating a human fence around the stage. Caya couldn't believe all of the people that had turned out to see Holiday Barbie. The human fence was probably ten people deep for about forty yards all around the stage. Nick took Caya's hand and led her to the stage. Nick approached the microphone with Caya in tow. He put on his people pleasing smile and spoke with the voice of authority. "Welcome pack members. I hope your stomachs are full. Before we begin the games, I wanted to present to you a special, new member of the pack. Please meet Caya Braswell. I know you have all heard rumors of my bringing home a mate and I wanted you all to meet her. I know you will love her as much as I do. Please continue to enjoy yourselves with food and games. Caya would love to meet each of you if you would like to give her your personal welcome."

Nick led her off the stage. People started forming a single-file line. Nick bent and whispered in her ear, "They want to give you their well wishes. If there is a question you would rather not answer, you can always defer to me and I will answer for you. This will be painless. I promise." *Of course, you are not the one on trial here Mr. Defer to Me,* thought Caya.

Members of the pack took turns welcoming her. Her hand felt like it would was becoming raw from all of the handshaking. She much preferred the handshaking to the bear hugs that some of the men bestowed upon her.

One gentleman approached that Caya recognized. She couldn't believe her eyes. She cried, "Grandpa!" Nick looked at the gray haired man with some consternation. Grandpa gave Caya a hug, but it was not as obtrusive as some of the other hugs she had received recently. Caya asked, "What are you doing here?" Grandpa answered, "Well, the quick version of the story is that I was restless with my former pack and Nick was nice enough to take me in to the Puyallup pack." Caya's immediate response clued Nick in to how she knew Cayden Graves. "How does James feel about your defection?" Grandpa's only reply was that none of the family was too happy about it. Cayden Graves was James' grandpa. Caya wondered what happened to make him leave his pack. Caya had learned from Nick that werewolf packs were extended families. They shared a family bond that human families never experienced. Despite Caya's interest in the situation, she was overjoyed to see someone with whom she had a relationship outside of a few days.

As grandpa left Caya to greet her other guests, a young woman about Caya's age, with long blonde hair and bright blue eyes abruptly grabbed Caya's arm at the elbow. At the woman's touch, Caya felt an alarming reluctance to look the woman in the eye. Suddenly, visions began to appear in Caya's mind, visions of this woman with Nick. Nick was smiling at the stranger, hugging her, and kissing her quite intimately. There were more visions intruding upon Caya's thoughts, visions of them picnicking on top of a large hill with wildflowers. Caya tried to block the images, but she didn't know how. She was shaking uncontrollably. Nick wrapped his arms around her as he yelled for Seth. Nick whispered for Caya's hearing only, "Honey, whatever she just showed you, just remember that you are my mate and you are the only one for me." Caya couldn't respond. Her continued shaking was only getting worse. The urge to break free of Nick's embrace was overwhelming. The home videos that were forced into Caya's mind would not retreat. She wanted to kill that woman. *Where is this coming from? I am not a violent person.* Seth was beside Nick in no time. Nick was telling him to take Denae home and stay with her and not to let her out of his sight until Nick arrived to talk to her. Seth left in hot pursuit of this Denae person.

Caya was overwhelmed with anxiety. Her breaths were getting shallower and shallower. She could feel her insides begging for her to change forms. Nick began to whisper to her again, "Babe, please don't change forms right now. I know you are upset, but focus on me. Focus on what I am telling you. You-Are-The-Only-Woman-For-Me. The relationship I had with Denae was over the minute I found you." Caya opened her mouth to speak, "Nick, Nick, I feel like my insides are tearing me apart." Nick pulled her into a bear hug unlike the others she had experienced that night. "I know baby. You are doing great. Continue to focus on me holding you. My pack family is a little worried that you are unstable. Now is not the time to prove them right. Try your best to keep it together. I will get you out of here real soon, but they need to see that you can control your emotions, that you will not go off on a killing spree." Caya looked up into Nick's concerned face and said, "That is exactly what I want to do."

Tears started forming in her eyes. Nick continued to comfort and encourage her. Eventually, Caya was able to wipe the tears from her eyes and put a semi-smile on her face. Nick's relief was very evident when his broad shoulders began to relax a little. Caya noticed that Halina, Felicia, Aaron, and Will had made a barrier between Caya and the audience. Felicia took Caya's hand and said, "Well done sister." Caya looked down at her hand and noticed only peach fuzz on it and that fuzz was beginning to retreat. Caya put on a brave face, walked passed Halina and her entourage and continued to greet her audience.

Nick couldn't believe his good fortune. This could have turned out totally different and he was so thankful that it hadn't turned into the event that would have made her life here in Puyallup a lot harder. After a few greetings, Nick spoke to the crowd. "As you all have witnessed one of our pack has tried to undermine my mate's resolve. Caya has shown just how resilient and capable she is to stand by an Alpha. I WILL not tolerate anyone trying to hurt her. Denae will suffer the consequences of her actions. Caya is part of your pack now and I expect each and every one of my pack members to respect and protect her. With that said, you can imagine tonight's event has taken a toll on her so if you will excuse us we are going to retire. Please continue to enjoy your games and on behalf of Caya and myself thank you for sharing this time with us."

Caya couldn't help but notice the same sort of authoritative tone in Nick's voice that she had noticed earlier, but this time it was tinged with a little bit of threat. She was warmed by the way he wished to protect her. However, she felt she would become unhinged if he left this evening to go see his former girlfriend. It didn't matter to her whether it was to render some judgement upon her or not. *I can't believe this feeling of jealousy is so strong. I barely know this guy and a few minutes earlier I was ready to kill for him. This is not me. I think the animal in me is taking over more and more each day.*

Nick led Caya to the house. Once they were in the safety of his home Nick could see the consternation written all over her face. "A penny for your thoughts?" was his question. Caya, who had been staring at the wooden floorboards of the house, slowly lifted her leaden head to look Nick in the eye. Tears started forming again. "I wanted to kill her once she put those images in my head. I thought I could change and run after her and tear her to shreds. That is not me! I am losing myself to this animal that I have become!"

Nick pulled her close and placed a kiss on the top of her head and then locked that kiss in place by placing his chin on that exact spot. When he spoke, his words were full of emotion, the type of emotion that is usually followed by a waterfall of tears. "I could not be more proud of you Caya. I know you are upset and may not really know the extent of your emotions right now, but you just proved that you have complete control of your wolf. Your wolf is there to protect you. She would have taken over and probably killed Denae had you allowed her reign. You just showed the pack and I that when you need to, you can take control of the animal inside you. Now, you just need to learn how to coexist with her. Despite what you may think, you are still you and that is the woman I love. It took great strength to show restraint tonight.

I am not sure exactly what Denae showed you, but I can pretty well guess and if the tables were turned, even with my experience keeping my wolf at bay, I am not sure I could show that much restraint." Nick removed his chin and Caya looked up into those emerald gems that she was growing to love. Her words were broken and quiet, "Thank you for talking me down tonight. If you hadn't been there for me, I am not sure that tonight wouldn't have turned out differently. I have one more request of you tonight." Nick raised his right eyebrow in question. Caya continued, "Please do not go to her tonight." Nick looked her in the eye and said, "I am here all night. She can wait. I need to cool off before speaking to her anyway. If I don't, I may take up the task you wanted to do earlier."

Chapter 8

Alpha and mate spent the rest of the evening watching the new episode of the *Bachelor*. When Caya retired to her room for the night, Nick kissed her forehead and told her one more time how proud he was of her. As Caya lay in bed, she couldn't help thinking how she was going to confront Denae. She wasn't sure what Nick had in store for his ex, but she knew as long as they lived on the reservation together she would come in contact with Denae again. This was not a pleasant thought and kept Caya awake for several more hours tossing and turning in her bed. When she awoke the next morning, she showered and dressed and by the time she made it to the kitchen she realized that everyone had eaten breakfast and started their day's tasks. She didn't realize that she had overslept, but was not at all surprised since she had trouble falling asleep last night.

Since she couldn't feel Nick's presence, she assumed he was paying a visit to Denae. *If only I could be a fly on the wall during that conversation. On second thought, that might not be a good idea.* She wasn't at all sure that she could keep her composure the next time she was around Denae. After cleaning up after breakfast, Caya climbed the stairs to the third floor library. She had been interrupted the other day before she was able to find the book for which she was searching. She went back to the box she had started unloading and found *Shiver* at the bottom. Why is everything at the bottom when you need it? She hoped by reading this book she would have a better insight to her werewolf life. Surely, the books were not all fiction.

Nick found Caya huddled in the corner with a book. She looked up from her reading as he walked in the doorway. He felt drained after dealing with Denae and although he could sense her concern and curiosity as to what had taken place he could tell that she would wait for him to fill her in on the visit when he was ready. He was flummoxed as to how quickly they were able to read and sense each other's emotional state. Like Caya, learning the particulars of being mated to someone was new to Nick as well. He may be more familiar with werewolf life, but they were even in their knowledge bank when it came to mates. The sea of her eyes, helped calm him and his wolf.

When he had arrived at Denae's cottage, where she lived with her younger brother, he had wanted to rip her to shreds. His wolf was only cajoling him into the act. Just as he was prepared to protect Caya, his wolf was every bit as prepared to protect her wolf. Nick hoped that Caya and her wolf would become one soon. That was the only way that she would feel at peace with her new life. As Nick approached Denae, he had sensed her fear. Although she smelt of fear, he also could detect her feeling of triumph, which only irritated Nick more. As Nick came closer, Denae looked at the floor in submission to her Alpha. "Denae I don't care what pictures of us you placed in Caya's mind, but you know that what you did not only endangered her, but you and the rest of our pack. That is punishable by death. We have discussed that the pack is not comfortable with your witchcraft and you are not to use it if you live among us. The use of your mind tricks is also punishable by death when used on an Alpha or his mate." As Nick spoke, red consumed his neck and face. Denae could almost imagine steam coming from his ears. "What do you have to say in your defense?"

Denae looked up in those green eyes she loved and pleaded her case. "Nick, all I can say is jealousy overtook me at the time that I met your mate. Just a few days ago, we were seeing each other and perhaps you were not as involved in our relationship as I. I have grown to care deeply for you and I couldn't stand the fact that you had found your mate and left me high and dry." Denae looked back to the floor as Nick responded to her comments. "You are not to call me anything but Alpha, as our relationship has changed. Just because we had a relationship at one time does not give you liberties to address me so intimately, nor does it give you the right to this teenage jealousy. You were born a werewolf. You know as well as I that we can have intimate relationships, but our life is with our mate. You were just a distraction until I found my mate. If you are heartbroken, that is your fault for not remembering your place in the hierarchy. Because I understand to an extent that you are full of female emotion, I will spare your life and in return you will leave this pack and search for a home with another wolf pack. Should I be contacted for references, I will let the Alpha know that you left of your free will and that you and I had a relationship that was extinguished when I found my mate. You had grown so attached to me that you needed space to come to terms with my mate's existence within the pack.

You will have one week to find a place and move your household to your new home. If you wish to leave your things behind, I will send your brother with them once you are settled. You are not to have any contact with me or Caya during this transition period or thereafter. Are we clear?" Still staring at the floorboards, Denae replied, "Yes, Alpha." Nick backed away and as he did he asked, "Can I trust you to follow my orders or do I need to keep a guard on you at all times until you leave the property?" With tears trailing down her cheeks, Denae responded, "You can trust me Alpha." Nick nodded to Seth and as they were headed out the door Nick turned to look at Denae once more and said, "Denae, this was not personal. You understand our ways. You knew we would only be together until we tired of one another or our mates came along. Fortunately, I have found mine and I hope you will find your mate soon." Denae spoke between sobs, "Congratulations Alpha." The windows on the cottage rattled in their casements as Nick slammed the door of the cottage. Seth spoke reverently to his Alpha, "That was humane of you to spare her life Alpha." With head bowed, Nick kept walking toward home as he replied, "Thanks brother, but I need to show Caya that werewolves can show mercy and aren't always animalistic."

Caya's voice broke through Nick's thoughts as she said, "Rough day?" Nick placed a half smile on his face for her benefit as he approached her corner and slid down the wall to sit beside her. "I will be glad to tell you about it later. I just want to sit here in quiet for a few minutes if you don't mind." Caya laid her head on Nick's shoulder as she responded, "Quiet has become my healing medicine and it sounds as if you need that now." They sat in that corner not uttering a word to one another, but yet comforting each other all the same. Nick broke their meditation when he commented, "We have to get you some furniture in here. I am not sure my butt can handle too many of these moments of solitude." Alpha and mate looked at each other and began to laugh and heal.

It was two days before Nick could relate what happened with Denae to Caya and she never pushed him for answers. He could see her relief when he told her that his ex was banished rather than dead. Caya wasn't sure whether her relief came from the humane justice that Nick had rendered or the fact that deep down Caya wanted to put an end to her rival's life herself. She prayed that it was her humanity that was the answer to that query. Caya was not at all sure that becoming one with her wolf wouldn't mean that she would lose more of her humanity. This conflict is what created the trench that was dividing her from the werewolf world.

While Nick attended to his job and pack business, Caya found herself continuing to unpack her belongings and setting up her library. Will had finished the bookcases and Caya busied herself with unpacking books and placing them on the shelves. Furniture had been ordered for the reading area. With her belongings in place, she felt more at home in the house. She was still adjusting to the comings and goings of people she didn't know through the house. She found solace with Felicia, Nick's sister. Felicia would check to see if she wanted to go shopping or for a walk on the grounds. She even told Caya some of the pack history. Caya learned that Nick's father ruled with an iron hand and Nick was determined to rule the pack from a more nurturing perspective. However, Caya felt that Nick could use the iron hand if needed. Although Nick and Caya were spending less time together as they did when she first arrived, Nick always ate dinner with her and afterward they went for a run in their wolf forms.

It was still very painful for Caya to change forms and she was still reluctant, but she had been told that it would become easier the more she melted into this way of life. When she tired of unpacking, she would read or enjoy Halina's, Nick's mother's, flower garden. She would help

Halina in the kitchen, but cooking was not her forté. She always volunteered to clean up after the meals. Tidying up was her strong suit.

As the days progressed she found that she was missing her teaching job. At some point, there would be no more unpacking and she had no idea how she would spend her time. She didn't know how to broach the topic with Nick. She was better about controlling her changes to her wolf so she wasn't as nervous about getting out of the house. When she became restless while reading on the balcony, she would peer at the woods and think how she would love to change and go for a run. Although Nick allowed her to walk around the estate, he still required her to take he, Halina, or Felicia if she was going to stray too far from the house.

The weather was particularly nice one day and Halina was busy in the kitchen cooking lunch. Felicia had gone into town to buy a few groceries for her mother, and Nick was held up in his office with some of the pack members. Caya decided she wanted to explore more of the wooded area around the lake. She set off on her own traipsing through the wildflowers as they blew in the slight breeze that had made its way through the forest.

She never came to the woods in her human form. She and Nick were always allowing their wolves full reign when they went to the woods. The wooded area looked very different from her human perspective. Although her senses were keen in her human form, they were not as intense as she found them to be in her wolf form. The foliage was not as bright, the sounds were not as prominent, and the feel of the ground beneath her feet was not as textured. She realized that when she embodied her wolf she was at one with nature; as a human she was somewhat distanced from nature in a way only the werewolf world would understand. As she was embracing this epiphany, she noticed movement out of her peripheral vision and was shocked into awareness as a piercing howl caused her to look in the direction of the movement and howl.

Standing to her right, on the same side of the lake, no more than fifty yards away stood a yellow haired wolf, with blue eyes and teeth bared. It quickly occurred to her that Nick didn't want her to come alone whether it was because of the danger to her or from her. At this moment, she had deduced the danger was to her. You didn't have to be a werewolf long to understand aggression. Caya couldn't recall having seen this wolf in the woods before; yet there was something vaguely familiar about it. Panic had set in and Caya did the only thing she could do in such a circumstance and that was change into her wolf form and run. For once, she did not hesitate to change, nor did she notice the agony it usually caused because her wolf took over and instinct set in.

Part of her humanity must have been in control as she was certain that complete wolf instinct would have been to fight. Racing through the underbrush, jumping a fallen tree, Caya ran for her life as the aggressive wolf pursued her. Caya was at a disadvantage as she was less familiar with this area compared to her aggressor.

Distance was decreasing rapidly between the wolves as Caya came to an abrupt stop before a very old, dilapidated cabin. Once her human form was restored, she made a vow to push herself harder on the treadmill to give herself an edge during future encounters. She hastily ran inside the cabin and frantically looked for something to barricade the door. If this had been *Little House on the Prairie*, there would be a wooden bar that would secure the door. Unfortunately, this is not television and is the wrong time period. Half of this cabin's rusted, metal roof had collapsed and it was evident that the only occupants for many years had been opossums and other rodents.

As Caya continued to look about her for something to brace the door, the door flung open and in walked Denae. Her squinty eyes and hard set mouth identified her as not being in a friendly mood. Caya retreated further in the cabin and placed the one piece of furniture still residing within the cabin a handmade, wooden table between her and her agressor. Caya was scared stiff, literally. It was the maniacal smile that evidenced Denae's unbalanced psyche. *Has she gone mad? I understand jealousy, but I think my presence in Nick's life has left her unhinged much like the lower part of the door that I was unsuccessful in barricading. What are my options? I am a lover not a fighter. Unlike the damsels in distress in my novels, my hero has no idea where I am located so that he might rescue me. Why did I not listen to Nick's apprehension about my entering the forest alone?*

Although Caya may not be a born fighter and may be scared beyond comprehension, she had watched plenty of television. She just relied on what she did know even if it wasn't instinctual. She would try to calm her nerves in order to open her mouth and converse with her nemesis, easier said than done. Her knees were shaking, and she had broken out in a sweat. Her heart felt like it would jump out of her chest. Where was that blasted wolf instinct when you needed it?

All the while Caya was contemplating the error of her ways and what to do to extricate herself from this situation, Denae was shuffling from one foot to the other trying to get around the table and reach Caya. Caya noticed a poker next to the stone fireplace. If she could make it to the purposed weapon in time, she might appear to be a more formidable adversary. She couldn't shake the fear that if she moved too far from the table she would become Denae's captured prey. Caya and Denae started to parry as if boxers around the table, keeping the obstacle between them. Apparently, Denae was into toying with her prey, as it was obvious to the prey that her pursuer could cross the top of the table at any time and end this in one fell swoop. Glancing around the room, looking for some escape, Caya was unsuccessful in thinking clearly in her present situation.

The predator could sense the prey's fear and this only heightened the hunt for her. She gave a slight maniacal smile and lifted one leg onto the table. The prey decided to run for the poker. Denae was on top of her as her hand wrapped around the cold piece of metal. They both plummeted to the floor. Pinned to the floor and the breath knocked out of her, Caya was at Denae's mercy. Adrenalin set in and Caya was able to lift the poker enough to hit Denae. She could not tell where she hit her immediately. Fortunately, the blow was enough to make Denae roll off her body and she quickly stood poker still in hand. The jilted foe was holding her head. Blood was running down her face.

Guilt crept onto Caya like a cowboy to his horse. She didn't want to hurt this person. She was just trying to stay alive and at present she felt her life was very much in danger. *I have to diffuse this situation, but how? I have to calm her and let her see that I am not a threat to her, but clearly I am. The guy she loves is my mate and has just exiled her from her family.* Denae was in a seated position on the floor in front of the fireplace still holding her head. Caya backed away slowly making her way to the open door. She should be making her escape, but empathy clothed her and she stopped and willed her mouth to open. "We need to get you to the main house so we can tend to your wound." With one eye and the wound above it covered with her hand, the victim of the blow opened her right eye and glared at Caya. "I will heal quickly and when this room stops spinning you will no longer be a part of Nick's life," spurted his former female interest.

"Well that blow to the head did not knock any sense into you," egged on Caya. "You have been a werewolf all of your life. Unlike me, you have known no other life, but this one. Therefore you know that werewolves pursue their mates. Take a minute to look deep within and you will know that Nick is not your mate." Suddenly, a voice interrupted Caya's thought process. Nick's voice was so clear. "Caya where are you? Think about where you are located. Let me see what is around you, through your eyes," the voice commanded. *How on earth do I communicate my location to him? Why can I hear his voice in my head?* While Denae was still incapacitated, Caya allowed her thoughts to describe the area where she was being held hostage. She thought of the abandoned cabin with its rusty, metal roof and barely hinged door. She thought of the sight of Denae trying to get to a standing position. She hoped that those thoughts were enough to get Nick to her quickly.

Caya resumed her trained thought on the one-sided conversation with Denae. "Denae, why are you letting your hatred of me consume you like this? You know Nick doesn't love you and your mate is somewhere looking for you and yet you are wasting your time on me." Denae's brow furrowed as she looked straight at Caya. "You have no idea what your entrance into this pack has caused me!" spurted the wounded female. Caya decided she may want to speak in soothing tones if she wished to diffuse this encounter. Her voice soft and laced with sympathy,

Caya retorted, "I know you have been forced to leave your family. I know you want to be loved and the man you think you love is in love with someone else. You should be concentrating on finding happiness for yourself instead of dwelling on my presence in your life. Don't you want to find your mate?" Denae slid back to the floor, face covered with both hands now. Her body was being racked by sobs.

Nick had been conducting a business meeting in his home office when he felt his body shake with fear. Surrounded by his trusted pack, he knew he was in no danger so the fear must have been propelled down the link to him, the link he shared with Caya. The men noticed that Nick uncharacteristically fell silent and his face had a look of consternation about it. They fell silent and just watched the Alpha to see what he would do or say next. He looked up and bolted out the door with the council in hot pursuit of him. He ripped the door off its hinges and changed to his wolf form in mid-air as he leaped off the porch with the others following suit.

They raced for the woods and sure danger seemed to be eminent. When Nick reached the cabin, he changed into his human form just as he breeched the doorway. Caya looked up to behold all of the commotion to find Nick's normally emerald eyes blazing at the two women huddled on the rustic cabin floor. Nick was prepared for battle when the men entered the cabin, but they found Caya huddled over a sobbing Denae. Nick rushed to Caya's side and lifted her into his arms. He was so thankful to find that the blood on her clothes was not her blood, but rather his ex-girlfriend's. As Nick held Caya, she allowed her pinned up emotions to take over and she too started sobbing over Nick's bare upper torso. The entourage that had accompanied Nick to rescue Caya, man-handled Denae to force her to stand. With eyes closed, Nick took in the sweet smell of Caya's floral scent from the body wash she used. Continuing to take in the feel of her body against his, he asked, "Are you ok?" Caya simply sniffed and nodded her head in affirmation.

Nick reluctantly opened his eyes as Seth was headed for the door with the perpetrator who threated his mate's very existence. His gaze bore into Denae as he swore, "You have lost the gift of freedom that I bestowed on you the other day. I felt sorry for you then, but now all I feel is contempt for you!" Seth halted his progress to allow Denae to look and speak to the Alpha. In between sobs, Denae begged for Nick and Caya's forgiveness and told them how sorry that she was. Seth pushed her through the doorway. Caya separated from Nick and yelled, "Seth, wait!" Seth looked from Denae to Nick with disbelief in his eyes. Nick nodded in assent for Seth to await him just outside the cabin.

Caya pleaded with Nick. "Nick, please have mercy on her again. She was consumed with jealousy, but I really think she is repentant this time. I looked into her eyes and found self-loathing there. I think she just feels she has lost everything and that brought out the evilness I just witnessed. I believe I was able to talk her down and she will leave now in search of her mate. She accepts that we are mates and even if I weren't in the picture she had no chance with you." Nick grabbed Caya by the shoulders. "Did she not just try to kill you? I could feel your fear through our link. It is because you housed such emotion that you were able to hear me through our link so clearly and were able to lead me to your location. She not only put your life in danger she was going to end it for you!

I cannot remain Alpha if I cannot levy justice on my own people." Nick's strained voice actually scared Caya a little. She could only imagine what he would do to someone that threatened her life. In response to this thought, she pleaded with Nick not to end a life if for no other reason other than to save her own sanity because she could not live knowing that she was the cause of Denae's demise. "At least wait until you have calmed down before emitting justice. I am beginning to understand that as Alpha you have certain responsibilities and keeping the pack safe is one of those, but you know females run on emotion. She was just blinded by that emotion for a bit. I helped her to see that. If I had truly feared for my life in the end, I would have killed her, but I see the good in her and I couldn't bring myself to do it and I don't want you to do it for me. Was the real threat not to me? Someday I will be co-Alpha to this pack. Let me show that I can show mercy when incidents necessitate." Nick just stared at her in disbelief. "How am I blessed with such an awesome if not crazy mate?" was his only reply as he physically turned her and they left the musty, dilapidated cabin.

Chapter 9

Several days passed and Nick would not tell Caya of Denae's fate. As a matter of fact, Nick would not talk about the incident at all. His mood had definitely changed and he was spending a lot of time held up in his office with the pack council. Now that Caya had her things unpacked, furniture in place, library and offices finished, boredom was overtaking her. She was setting in her rocking chair, on the balcony of her office, when Nick came in search of her. He sat in a lounge chair next to her and they watched the sunset before going down for dinner. Finally, Caya broke the silence, "Do you think we could go pick up my car and allow me to visit with Rayna tomorrow? I have not mauled anyone since I have been here and the one time I probably would have been justified in taking a life I didn't. Would you think about letting me off my leash just a little?" Nick continued to look toward the skyline contemplating. After what seemed an eternity he replied, "I am sure that Rayna would love to see you and I sense your restlessness. You call and see if she is available and I will take you for a visit." Caya felt a little victorious when she asked, "um, what about my car?" Nick chuckled, "You will have transportation to and from your destination. I am not holding you hostage." That remark hit a little close to home for both of them due to recent events. After another brief silence, Nick was texting away on his phone. He continued to send and receive messages as Caya called her bestie to see if they could hang the following day. Rayna was glad to hear from her former roomie. Rayna was excited about the opportunity to see Caya and catch up on each other's lives. Since Caya had moved onto the pack reservation they had not communicated.

The next day, as promised, Nick dropped Caya at her former apartment so she could spend some quality time with Rayna. Caya was a little confused when Seth tagged along, but she just figured that the guys had some business in Tacoma while she was hanging with her girl. She and Rayna talked, ate at their favorite restaurant, and did a little shopping at the mall. When they returned to the apartment complex Caya realized her car was missing. "Rayna, what happened to my car?" Rayna's response was not what Caya was expecting. "Nick sent some guys over to pick it up. Is it not at your mansion, as you call it?" Steam was rolling off of Caya as she responded, "I haven't seen my car since I moved." Rayna was perplexed. "I guess that explains why Nick brought you over here." Caya knew she had to control her emotions before she started changing to her wolf form. She had not told Rayna about her new abilities and Nick would not let her out again if she ruined this opportunity even if he was the cause of her frustration.

Nick was right on their agreed upon time for pick up. When Caya met him at the truck and slammed the door as she lifted herself inside, he knew something was wrong. "Did you and Rayna get into an argument?" Caya's reply was short and forced. "No." Nick thought, *uh oh, I have done something to set her off, but what? We have not been together the better part of the day.* Nick started driving and they refrained from conversation until they were almost home.

Caya spoke first. "Where is my car?" Nick kept his eyes on the road in front of him. He grinned as he said, "Oh, you noticed that it was missing did you? Well, I had the guys sell it." Caya went rigid in her seat. "You sold my car without my permission. Nick, just because we are more or less engaged doesn't mean you have total autonomy over me and my possessions. I loved my Oldsmobile Cutlass Supreme."

Nick thought she was about to start throwing punches so he pulled off to the side of the road. He turned in his seat and looked into those hazel eyes that today appeared green like his. "It was a decent car and in its prime was probably a cute red sports car, but I was a little reluctant to let you continue to drive it because it didn't sound very reliable when the guys picked it up for me." Caya twisted a little further in her seat until she could lean over and get face to face as if to kiss him. However, a kiss is not what he received. With lips pursed she said, "You didn't think you needed to consult me on this matter. You think it is fine for you to uproot me from my home and friends, plant me in unfamiliar territory, and get rid of my means of transportation!" It was apparent that Nick's patience was wearing a little thin. He started the truck and looked down the road as they continued to their destination. When he spoke, he had a no nonsense tone. "I would have consulted with you about the matter, but it would have ruined my surprise."

As they pulled up to the house, a brand new Dodge Charger was sitting out front. Caya's eyes got as big as Frisbees. She asked, "Who drives that rad Charger?" Nick started guffawing. Once he could speak again, he said, "I hope you will." Caya jumped out of the truck before Nick could put it in park. She ran in front of the truck to get to the tantalizing gift that Nick was apparently bestowing on her. When Nick got out of the truck and made his way to her, she was all smiles again. "You really bought this for me?" Nick opened the driver side door as he said, "Yep." Caya was too excited to make any response other than, "Cool." The black Dodge Charger had a wide royal blue stripe down the center from one end to the other end of the car. The interior was a medium gray, all leather. Caya was so overcome with joy tears started rolling down her cheeks. Nick squatted down outside the car while she tried out the driver's seat. Concern was earmarked all over his face. "You don't like the inside?" Caya looked at him and smiled, "I love all of it! Does this mean I don't get a ring?" Nick chuckled and leaned inside the car to kiss her. This kiss was their first really passionate kiss and it took them both by surprise. Nick stood and pulled her from the car. Staring into her eyes, he answered, "I am prepared to give you both and more." As they kissed again, Caya was thinking that as much as she loved the car she still wasn't sure if she was ready for a future with Nick. Caya remembered that she had not seen Seth when Nick picked her up. "Where is Seth?" Nick grinned again and said, "What do you think we were doing today? Who do you think drove this beauty home?" Question answered.

The next day, Caya couldn't wait to drive her new car. Nick had another meeting so he sent Felicia with her for the test drive. Caya may have scared Felicia a little with the speed, but they arrived back to the house in one piece. When they arrived, Nick met them in the hallway and asked Caya to join him in his office. Caya didn't miss the serious look upon his visage. When she entered the office, she noticed Seth and his brother Will. Seth was standing at the right hand of Nick as usual, but Will was seated in front of Nick's desk. Nick motioned for her to have a seat as well. Will greeted Caya and Caya responded in kind.

Caya really liked Will. They worked well together planning the furniture for the library and office upstairs. Nick cleared his throat. Caya noticed the furrowed brow as he spoke. "Caya, I have asked Will if he will act as your bodyguard and trainer. I know that you two have a good rapport and I trust him with your training and most importantly your life." Caya looked dumbfounded. *What training and why on earth should I have a bodyguard?* Nick could sense the onslaught of verbal communication that was fixing to come from Caya so he wisely asked the other two men to leave them for a bit to discuss matters. Caya was very thankful for that reprieve.

After closing the door to his office, he walked toward her and she stood, face red, and steam coming out her ears; he would have sworn. Caya was taking deep breaths to help her stay calm. It was not working. "Wh-Why do I need a bodyguard?" Nick tried to be calm and speak in soothing tones as not to rile her further, but this was non-negotiable for him so his words came out matter-of-fact. "There has already been one attempt on your life and there will be others because of your station in this pack. When I am unable to protect you, I need to know that you are somewhat versed in measures to protect yourself and that there will be someone who will protect you in my absence." Caya was a little taken aback. She had not thought about other people wanting to kill her. Would she ever understand this way of life? She swept past him in a blur, threw open the door and headed out of the house all the while yelling, "I do not need a babysitter." Nick noticed the guys sitting on the porch as he ran past them in chase of Caya who was headed for the woods, turning into a beautiful brown wolf when entering the lush green environment.

Will remarked, "I guess that did not go as planned?" Seth answered, "Well it depends how you thought it would go. I have gotten to know Caya pretty well since she came here and it went about as I expected. Don't worry. After they both calm down, she can usually see his point of view whether she wants to or not. Caya is smart and down to earth. She will see the need of your presence once he explains things in Caya's terms. She doesn't understand that there is a need for her to protect herself and to have other means of protection also if necessary." Will looked toward the woods. "And you think that he will make her see it?" Seth looked at Will. "They are mates. They are both learning what that means, but he has a way with her once he calms down and doesn't fly off the handle himself. I have to admit that I have never seen anyone that can unhinge him like she does. They will work it out. He just can't forget that he almost lost her a few days ago. He can't stand to think that it may happen again, not when he just found her."

By the time Nick had made it to the lake, Caya had already turned back to human form. He sensed that she was still unsettled and hurt. "I just want to know that you are safe. I almost lost you. I don't want you to be unprotected again. If you want me to let you have your independence, I have to know that you can defend yourself." Caya continued to look at the clear water in the lake. She focused on the fish swimming free among the rocks in the bottom. Ever since she had arrived here, she felt like a prisoner. Just when she felt she was being given some freedom, Denae caused her to become a prisoner again. *Why couldn't he have talked to me about this before? Why did he have to go full steam ahead and find me a bodyguard? True, he did take the time to choose someone I knew. He is just concerned about my welfare.*

Daggummit, she knew all of this, but she still felt like he was treating her like a child. Caya took deep breaths as she considered all of the facts and allowed her emotions to somewhat subside. She could feel him trying to calm her with his Alpha powers again. She turned abruptly and said, "Don't! I hate it when you do that. Let me work through this in my own way." After she stared at her bare feet for a few minutes, she continued. "I know you are worried about me and I really do appreciate that, even though because of my outburst you probably think I don't. I am very independent and this new way of life has not only taken me by surprise, but it has left me feeling like a prisoner. I can't see myself continuing to live like this. I want to find my niche, but I am floundering in my own lake."

She paused and Nick raised his hand to touch her shoulder. She pulled away and said, "No." She continued, "If I consent to let Will give me self-defense classes will you please grant me some independence?" Nick felt torn. He was torn between wanting to give her what she wanted and wanting to keep her safe. She had no idea the dangers that lurked around her, around both of them because he was the Alpha of the most coveted pack in Washington State. His only response was, "I will try."

After they left the lake, Nick showed her the workout garage at the back of the house. She noticed that it had weights, treadmills, stationary bikes, and boxing bags, on which she just might have to picture Nick's face right about now, and mats, for what, she did not know. She asked Nick how the mats were used. He relaxed then and smiled and sheepishly looked up at her and said, "That is where you and Will will wrestle." Caya's response was immediate, "What?!" Nick ran for the house with Caya in hot pursuit. He locked himself in his office with Seth and Will so Caya went upstairs to read. That would always help calm her. Unfortunately, her life was not working out like the lives of those people in her novels. No surprise there.

She and Will began a routine whereby after breakfast they would head to the garage. She would warm-up on the bikes or treadmill. Then, he would teach her some self-defense techniques. On the first day of class, Will asked Caya to show him how she would defend herself in certain situations. He would not tell her what he was going to do. He would just attack and she would have to respond. First, he was facing her and came at her and placed his strong hand on her left forearm. As she felt his fingers tighten around her arm, she instantly felt very self-conscious and uncomfortable with Will's hands on her. Her first response was to try to jerk her arm away. When he asked how that technique was working for her while putting her in a headlock, she reached up and slapped his face. His response had been to release her, which to Caya was the desired effect. Then, he caught her from behind and had his hulky arms wrapped around her and she would try turning her body back and forth hoping he would release her. He would inevitably get frustrated with what he called her "holding back" and say something or put her on her butt just to make her angry. That is when she would no longer hold back and give him everything she had.

She hated that he could pull her strings and get her dander up. That is when the slapping and kicking would start. On day two, Will grabbed her forearm again and told her to send an elbow flying to his nose. Caya turned pale. Will said, "Do it!" She complied with a quick jab with her right elbow, but Will turned his head so that the blow landed on the side of his face. "You have to do it harder, southern belle," was his retort. He grabbed her from behind and told her to kick back into his groin area. As she tried to lift her leg, he maneuvered his leg to cover the sensitive area before her foot planted itself.

For the first few days of training, she often came back to the house in the evening worn to a frazzle and bruised. She could see Nick's concern when she winced or collapsed on the couch and fell asleep, even with the guys in there watching television. They got to where when she entered and headed their way they would give up the couch and head for the recliner or other areas in the room. Nick could tell when they were feeling comfortable with her because they would just move to the floor in front of the couch. On these days, Nick would want to speak with Will immediately rather than wait on a weekly update of Caya's progress. If Caya had been awake long enough, she would often have heard their raised voices.

One day, Caya asked Will why Nick didn't take on the responsibility of teaching her self-defense. Will smirked and said, "Nick didn't think he could be tough enough on you." Caya responded, "Well, I guess you pat your own back all the way home thinking that you can toughen me up." Will kept his head down, but slowly raised his eyes to her and said, "I find it an honor to help you find your way here and I will always follow the orders of my Alpha. Plus, I have to admit I enjoy it when I can put you on your butt." Caya giggled, "Well, I admit I will feel accomplished when I put you on yours." Will took this as a challenge and said, "Bring it on girl, bring it on."

Weeks went by and Caya became stronger and more confident. When Will didn't have her practicing her self-defense moves, he had her running on the treadmill and lifting weights. One day, they took a break from the gym and he took her to the woods and explained how she needed to be aware of her surroundings and how to find a hiding spot if she were being pursued.

He pointed out thicker grass, gullies in the landscape, and mounds of boulders where she could barely squeeze between the rocks.

Another day, they walked around the house looking for items that could be used as weapons; scissors, knives, and a metal rod that was lying in the yard. Well at least she was staying busy for a portion of the day, but she still did not know how to fill the rest of her days. Nick seemed busy and preoccupied with pack business and once she finished training she was so tired she merely ate, showered, and went to bed.

However, this evening she was not tired as Will had cut training short because he had something else on his social calendar. She walked from the woods to the house and straight to Nick's office. His door was open and he was actually alone. She stood in the doorway staring at the hunched body over the desk. His hands were on either side of his head and he was looking down at the paperwork that littered the top of the desk. Not sure whether to proceed, she just stood there staring at him. He sensed her presence and looked up. Although he produced a smile for her, his visage was very haggard and the frown lines between his eyes were quite pronounced. She could tell there was deep concern and she didn't know how to respond to his appearance.

With eyes locked on to her, he stood and walked around the desk toward her as he asked, "Are you going to come in or just stand there holding up the door frame?" Caya took a step forward still unsure how she should respond to him. She stammered, "Are you busy?" *What a stupid question. You can clearly see he has a lot on his mind. Why are you still so uncomfortable being around him?* As she continued to non-verbally talk to herself, she noticed Nick seemed unsure of what he needed to do next as well. Eventually, he replied, "I am never too busy for a visit from you. I know I have not spent much time with you lately, but there is a major issue brewing and I have had to give this issue a lot of attention."

He held his hand out and Caya took it as he led her to a chair in front of his massive oak desk that had all of the detail of the woodwork that appeared throughout the house, definitely Will's handiwork. Nick perched on the edge of his desk facing Caya. "To what do I owe this visit? I see you are walking on your own accord so Will must have taken it easy on you today." Caya was still disturbed that this usually in control man seemed unsure of what to do about this pack issue and it really had him worried, which in turn now had Caya concerned.

Caya responded, "Yes, we were looking for hiding places again today. We went a little deeper in the woods and then he practiced scenarios on me. I thought I would like this better, but I think I want to go back to the gym." With frown lines deepening further, "Caya, do I need to speak to him? Do you need a break? He says you are progressing well and I don't see why you can't have a day off from training." Caya jumped up from her seat. "No, don't do that. He will think I am wimpy again. I am fine. I was just making conversation. Everything is fine. However, I would like to know why all of this training is necessary? Why am I in so much danger? Can't I just change and fight in wolf form? I might not be as reluctant if you would explain this situation to me rather than thrusting me into training."

Nick also stood and ran his hand through his hair. He walked away from her only to turn around and return to stand looking down upon her very confused face. "I can't today Caya. I will take time to discuss this with you, but I just can't do it today. Please just believe me when I say it is necessary." Caya continued to look into those emerald gems that always captivated her. "I didn't interrupt you when I came to the door because I could see you were very concerned about something. What can I do to help you? Talk to me Nick."

Suddenly, there was a rap on the opened door. They both turned to see Seth standing there not knowing whether or not to enter. Nick looked from Seth to Caya. "We will talk about this tomorrow, not because I don't want to take time to explain it today, but because I have to work some things out. Give me just a little time. By the way, training with Will is how you are helping me right now. Please don't run him off yet." The last part he said with a grin on his otherwise worried face.

Caya could tell he was trying to be light hearted, but she wasn't falling for it. She just stepped around the chair and walked toward Seth and the door. Once she arrived, Seth stepped aside to let her pass, but before she went out of the office, she turned to Nick and said, "Tomorrow. No excuses." Then, she walked through the doorway and headed for the stairs. She heard Nick say, "Tomorrow. No excuses." With that, Caya headed to the sanctuary of her library.

Nick told Seth to come in and close the door. Seth could see the same signs of worry that Caya had noted in Nick's appearance. Nick filled Seth in on the phone call he had received late yesterday. He told him that the Mount Rainier pack had lost their Alpha. There was dissension in the pack. It was up to him to lay claim to the pack and make them part of his pack. However, that would require that he go to the Mount Rainier commune and lay claim and set everyone in order. There was nothing worse than a werewolf pack without strong leadership. Since the Puyallup pack was the closest, it was up to him to bring unity and peace to the fragmented wolf pack.

He knew that this trip would take about a week, if not longer, to set everything right. Well, maybe not exactly right, but on the road to being right. Seth told him he would get the council together for a meeting after dinner. Nick thanked him and went back to his paperwork. Seth pulled out his cell phone and started making calls to everyone on the Puyallup council. When an emergency meeting was called, everyone forgot their plans and made arrangements to meet with their Alpha. Each member knew that Nick did not call emergency meetings, unless there were truly emergencies. Nick was a leader who was very respectful of family time, which was ironic since Nick did not have a family of his own yet. This was something that Nick had learned from the previous Alpha, his father. His father ruled with an iron hand, but he also valued his family and in that respect Nick continued to value that as well.

Nick went to get Caya from her library for dinner. That night at the dinner table was quiet but for the clanging of silverware, even the chewing of food seemed nonexistent. Everyone sensed the heavy weight that Nick carried on his shoulders. Caya helped clean up after dinner while the men went into the office for the council meeting. Caya decided that the weight she was feeling must be from the bond she shared with her mate. His worry became her worry even though she had no idea what was happening. When she went to bed, Nick's office door was still shut and no one had entered or exited.

Caya had not slept well. She tossed and turned all night. When she awoke and readied herself, she wondered what the day would hold. She was helping Halina place food on the table when she heard a commotion outside. She peeked out the window and saw a small boy being caroused by some of the youngsters of the pack. As she was watching the boy, she realized she recognized him. It was James' nephew, Emit. Caya ran out of the house and toward Emit. "Let him through. He is here to see me." The youngsters parted so that Caya could breech the mob that had formed by now.

Emit, a boy of nine years, ran to Caya and wrapped his scrawny arms around her waist. Caya kissed the top of his head and then stooped down so they were face to face. "Emit, what are you doing here? Where is your uncle James?" Caya looked around the boy searching for James' truck. She didn't see any sign of him anywhere around them. Emit spoke in quiet tones, "I had to see you. I had to know you were alright. Mom, Dad, nor Uncle James would bring me to see you." Caya was stunned. Once she could speak, she replied, "Are you saying you made your way here on your own?"

Emit's gaze went to his dust covered boots. Caya's voice rose, "Do you have any idea how dangerous that was? You cannot be traveling on your own. You can't enter another werewolf pack territory on your own." Emit continued to look at his boots as he started to cry. Caya realized that she had no idea what he had encountered on his journey to Puyallup, but this mob of young wolves was enough to scare a nine year old in itself. She caught him up in her arms and held him close to her trying to console him. She felt Nick's presence. The scene must have caught his attention and everyone else's for that matter. She didn't care. She continued to console this young one in her arms.

At Nick's proclamation that everything was fine and everyone needed to get to school and work the mob dispersed. Little Emit's eyes rose to meet Nick's. The boy had stopped crying, but was still sniffing. Caya stood and backed away a little and turned to look from the boy to Nick. Nick held out his hand for Emit to shake. Emit scowled at Nick's hand and then looked up into his eyes and said, "Are you the one who took Caya?" Caya and Nick were taken aback by this young man's brassiness in the face of a powerful Alpha, who by the way was from an opposing wolf pack. Caya looked at Emit and said, "Nick didn't take me. I came here because I wanted to come here." *Well that was not entirely true. I was drawn to Nick, but at the time had no idea why.*

Emit looked at Caya and replied, "Why would you leave Uncle James to come here? Why would you leave me? They wouldn't let me see you so I just took off." Nick looked the boy over for a minute and then said, "That was not the best decision you could have made. However, I applaud your determination." Emit asked Caya, "Why didn't you call me? I would have tried to explain to you that I had to see you. I had to see that you were ok. I had to know you hadn't left me for good."

Caya's heart broke for this little boy. They had grown close when she dated James. They would ride bikes together, and play catch. James would bring him to Caya's apartment and they would watch super hero movies together. She had not stopped to think how this change would affect Emit. She felt very guilty. She did not know what to say to him. Suddenly, she heard a vehicle barreling down the gravel drive to the house. When she looked up she knew what she would see, James' truck. As James exited the truck and headed their way, Seth, Will, and some others were exiting the front porch and headed his way. Nick motioned for them to stop and allowed James to get closer.

James started screaming at Emit, "Emit Raines what were you thinking taking off like that? Your mom and dad are sick with worry about what might have happened to you!" Emit had turned to see his uncle and then just as quickly started crying again at his angry words. He planted his face back into Caya's shirt which was becoming drenched in nine year old tears. Caya looked at James and mouthed, "Stop." James stopped in his tracks. Nick pushed around

Caya and stormed at James. "What do you think you are doing using that little boy to get to Caya?!"

James prepared for the melee that he could sense was coming. Nick launched himself at James and planted his fist upside James' jaw. After James righted his head, he launched himself at Nick. All Caya could see were fists flying while she was keeping Emit from witnessing these two immature werewolves fighting it out in their human forms. Caya winced with each punch that was thrown, the sound thundering with every connection. She looked at Seth and said, "Do something to stop them before they kill each other!" Seth just grinned at Caya and said, "They're just playing around for your honor honey. They aren't killing each other. I am enjoying the entertainment."

Suddenly, James was on the ground and Nick was not letting up. Blood was pouring from both of their faces. Caya was getting scared that they would change to their wolf forms and someone's life would be at stake at that point. Finally, she had witnessed all she could stand and she yelled, "STOP this minute you mangy dogs!" Nick's fist stopped in mid-air. James turned his head to look at her. They were both shocked at not only the forcefulness of her tone, but her choice of words as well. Nick stood and gave James his hand to help him off the ground. James spat blood on the yard before replying, "For the record, I want Caya back, but I would never use my nephew to get her back. I am banking on the fact that you are not her mate and have just deluded her into thinking that you are and one day she will see your true colors and leave you."

Nick's eyes were glaring at James as he spoke. Caya just knew they would start pounding each other again, but Nick, reluctantly, walked away. As he passed Caya, she lifted Emit's little chin with her finger so that they were looking at one another. "Emit you should not have come out here on your own. Sometimes parents and uncles don't let us do things because they are dangerous and they don't want to see us get hurt. I know it would upset you to see your parents worry. You know they are worried about you right now. It is not like you just walked down the street. You traveled way too far on your own.

The next time you need to talk to me call me and we will talk or I will come to get you, but do not leave home again." Emit said, "Are you mad at me too?" Caya shook her head, "No, but I am scared of what could have happened to you." Caya looked toward James. "Can he stay with me for a little while?" James nodded his head. "I need to talk to him first and let him know that this is not reward for his behavior." Caya agreed and turned Emit and walked him over to James so they could have a man-to-man conversation about the error of his ways.

While they talked, Caya walked back to stand beside Nick, but she couldn't ignore the concern James had for his nephew. He was holding him gently by the shoulders as he was reading him the right act. She could see the worry all over James' face. Once they had finished their heart-to-heart, he walked Emit back to Caya. "I will pick him up after lunch if that is ok with you?" Caya stated that she could bring him home, but that did not sit well with Nick. There was no way he would allow her to enter into the Tacoma pack alone and he was busy preparing to resolve the Mount Rainier issue. She had no clue as to the tension that having her here on the Puyallup reservation had created between the two packs. James agreed to pick Emit up after lunch. Caya pulled James to the side and reiterated to him that Emit needed time with her to see that she was ok and not being held against her will. James just nodded and headed toward the truck. His feelings were still too raw when it came to Caya.

Caya took Emit into the house where Halina plied him with more food than a growing boy could eat, even after his travels. Then, she walked him around the property and asked him about school. Before leaving, Emit made sure that Caya would still talk to him on the phone and come see him. She assured him that even though things were different between her and James that he was still going to be part of her life and she would continue to see him. When James picked him up after lunch, Emit seemed content and had promised Caya, in front of James, that he would not run off like that again for fear of making her mad next time.

Chapter 10

After dinner, Nick asked Caya if she wanted to go for a swim. After affirming that she would like that, they headed to the lake. When they arrived it was dusk, but quickly getting darker by the minute. Caya felt excited in a way she had not experienced before. As they swam and splashed each other, Caya felt their connection growing. There seemed to be a wildness about them both that she didn't understand. Nick grabbed her from behind and tried dunking her. Although she and Will had not practiced this scenario in water, she felt like showing off what she had learned in her self-defense training. She head-butted him, sank into the depths of the now chilling water, and grabbed his legs and sent him face first into the water as well. When she resurfaced, she looked around and didn't see Nick. She was starting to panic, thinking that her head butt might have left him unconscious and when she sent him head first into the lake could have caused him to drown. She dove into the water in search of him. It was dark now and they had disturbed the sandy bottom so it was impossible to even see her hands in front of her face. She tried feeling around for his body.

When she rose to the surface for air, he grabbed her again and pulled her close to him. After she shook the water out of her face, she realized they were eye to eye with the light of the full moon to Nick's back. She was a little worried about the serious look on his countenance. Then, he leaned in and kissed her. His warm lips were a contrast to the cool water in which they were submerged. When he released her mouth after a few minutes, she was in a bit of shock. She hadn't expected that. Nick laughed, "Why do you look so shocked? Well done by the way on the self-defense and the kiss." Caya felt her face turning every shade of red that she could fathom. She could feel her wolf and her body reacting to him and she couldn't decide whether she should pursue the passion or go for a run in her wolf form.

Her wolf beckoned to be let loose. Through the bond she had with Nick, she could feel his wolf's restlessness as well. "I am having trouble controlling my more animalistic half at the moment," stated Caya. Nick laughed and told her it was the full moon. He explained that it calls to their wolves and they demand to be released. It was not long after that pronouncement that they heard a pack of wolves running through the forest and howling at the full moon. Nick held her close and kissed the top of her head. "We will let our wolves have their reign, but we need to talk first," replied Nick. He continued, "That is if I can talk. Between the full moon and having you this close, all I want to do is take you to bed." Caya was stunned, not that he was thinking that. He was a male after all, but that he would just be so forthcoming with the information.

Caya didn't know how to respond. Nick spoke first, "I know we should wait until the bonding ceremony, but I am having a hard time controlling myself." Caya turned around in his arms and positioned them so that she had her back to him and they were facing the moon. She didn't know what she should say to him. Thankfully, he continued to speak while tightening his arms around her, "I guess that was a little forward? I know you can feel it too. I am learning about this bond between us just the same as you. I guess knowing that I am going to have to leave you for a while makes me want to get closer to you."

Caya took a moment to reflect on this. They stood and looked at the glowing moon and at the reflection it made on the surface of the lake. Nick did not push her for a response. Finally, Caya responded, "Where are you going?" Nick explained to her that the Mount Rainier pack had lost their Alpha and he needed to go provide leadership to an otherwise wanton pack. She felt lonely already. True Nick had not spent much time with her of late, but she could always feel his presence and go in search of him if she needed to see him. She questioned, "Can I not go with you?" His response was immediate, "No, it will be too dangerous for you to be there."

He turned her back around in his arms so that he could look her in the eye. "After the bonding ceremony, you will be able to attend more outings with me as my mate, but right now this trip will be too dangerous and I won't risk something happening to you." He placed another kiss on her lips and then he spoke again, "I will not rush you into sex. I know you may still not be fully comfortable with me." Caya stammered, "I need some more time. I do have feelings for you, but you may need to tutor me in that as well." Caya looked down so embarrassed that when her mate tried to lift her chin she forcefully resisted. Nick couldn't believe what he had just heard. "Are you saying that you and James never had sex?" Still looking into the lake Caya answered, "No."

Nick was silent for longer than he intended and tears started rolling down Caya's cheeks. He asked, "Are you a virgin?" Caya simply nodded her head in affirmation. It was Nick's turn to be stunned. Caya wasn't sure he was going to be able to respond. After what seemed like a lifetime, he responded, "Honey, I don't know how to thank you. It is very unusual for an Alpha to find a virgin mate. You saved yourself for me, your mate." Wrapping her tighter in his arms and then lifting her chin so she had to look into his eyes he said, "To find a mate our age that is a virgin is such a gift. You have honored me with the best gift a man could ask for. I promise to give you a mundane wedding where we incorporate the wedding of which you would have dreamed and the mating ceremony of my werewolf culture and no matter what it takes I will wait until that night for our bonding. That Caya is how I wish to honor you."

He bent his head and kissed her once again as if to seal his pronouncement. As he tried to wipe away her tears, she asked, "I thought you would be ashamed that I was still a virgin? I don't know what made me tell you like this. I guess I felt a little pressured." Nick responded, "I will never be ashamed of you. You honor me and when you feel I am pressuring you feel free to kick my butt." Caya laughed, "Don't forget that you just gave me permission." They both laughed as they stood in the lake bathed in the moonlight. When they left the lake, they changed into their wolf forms and joined the others running under the full moon. Caya couldn't ignore even in wolf form how close Nick stayed to her as if protecting her from the other males who may want to take her virginity.

The next day, as promised, they sat on the balcony of her office and discussed more about the mission on which Nick was soon to embark. He explained that as the closest Alpha he would have to go to the Mount Rainier pack and claim them as his pack. There would be dissention in the ranks, but they needed a leader that they could trust and he would have to prove to them that he was that leader. He also explained that word would spread fast that she was a virgin mate and that would put her in greater danger because all of the males would want to take her to be joined with them.

"You have no idea how coveted you are," he told Caya. Caya responded, "I thought you would think that I was silly and afraid and that was why I was still a virgin." Nick answered, "You are strong and loyal and that is why the other males will want you. I knew this about you before your revelation and that is why I needed you to be trained to defend yourself if necessary. Saving yourself for me is another way that you have proven that strength and loyalty.

I can't imagine how hard it will be for us to be apart. I need you to be strong while I am gone. I will try to be back within a week and during that time I need you to let Will shadow you constantly. Word is already spreading about your honor to me." Caya was flabbergasted. "What! You have already told the world that I am a virgin." Nick responded, "It is something to proud of. Don't be ashamed." "That is why everyone looked at me in awe at breakfast this morning," expounded Caya. Now it was Nick's turn to turn fifty shades of red.

"Promise me that you will not try to elude Will and you will follow his every command. His sole purpose while I am gone is to protect you." After a minute's hesitation, she shook her head in compliance with his wishes. "When will you leave?" she asked. "I must leave tomorrow. Mom and Felicia will be helping you make arrangements for the mating ceremony. I am not sure how much longer I can wait to bond with you. However, if you are not ready, I will not pressure you. You can set the date for whatever makes you comfortable and if you are not ready to set the date I will respect that as well." Caya decided that chivalry was not lost after all. It just may be a little hard to find.

The thought of Nick leaving for such an extended amount of time disheartened Caya. Although they had not been spending much time together as of late, she could always feel his presence and that was comforting to her. She did feel she was getting to know him better and there was no doubt that there was a connection between them like nothing she had ever felt before.

Changing into wolf form was getting easier as Nick had promised. It did still hurt to make the change, but it seemed to hurt a little less each time she tried it. She couldn't say she was one with her wolf yet. Her wolf often seemed to torment her wanting her to release the animal and give it complete control. Although she felt that tug all of the time, the full moon had brought about feelings within her she couldn't even explain. It was as if the moon was in control of her or her wolf rather. She was finding more strength to help her not succumb to the wolf, but her human side was not always in complete control. She still contemplated whether she wanted to be an Alpha's mate. With that title came much responsibility. She was so new to this way of life that she did not think that she could live up to the responsibility. However, she did know that a week without Nick on her compass was going to be very hard on her.

Nick had called a huge meeting in preparation for his departure. Caya knew Will was in the meeting, but she really wanted to take the opportunity to let her wolf run. She had so many pent-up emotions and feelings that she needed the escape. The night at the lake had really brought feelings to the forefront that Caya didn't realize she may have been harboring. She didn't like the control that mother-nature had over her. She hoped she could process some of this while Nick was away. The more she thought about his leaving the more anxious she became. She still didn't feel like this was her home. She was getting to know people and the way of life, but she still had times of unrest when she thought about living this way for the rest of her life. This was certainly not the life she had imagined for herself. She decided to change forms and take that run. She would not go far, but she needed to destress a bit. She was not gone more than thirty minutes.

When she exited the forest Seth was headed her way. "Seth, I am fine. I did not go far. I just needed to have a release. I stayed close. Will was in the meeting," pleaded Caya. As Seth drew closer Caya didn't notice a disgruntled look upon his face. She thought he was going to read her the right act about going into the forest alone. Seth drew up just short of her. "Well are you more relaxed? Last night was your first full moon. It is tough on a bred wolf, but I have no idea how you must have felt having been turned into a wolf in your adult years."

Did Caya detect empathy from this Beta of the pack? "Well, the run did help some. Thanks for asking. How was your meeting?" Seth looked at his feet, "I can't discuss that with you, but I will let you know that we have a game plan and I will protect our Alpha with my life." Caya inched closer to the hulking bodyguard and best friend of her mate. "Were you looking for me?" Seth looked her in the eye. "Yes. I need to explain how important it is that you not exert your independence while we are away. Do whatever Will tells you whether you agree with him or not. He is here to protect you, even if it is from yourself. This business is very important to the Alpha and he cannot be distracted worrying about you." Caya raised her eyebrows and took one step backward. "I see."

Caya was thinking very hard before she blew out what she actually wanted to say in response to his declaration. Why was he treating her like she was a wayward child? There was nothing wrong with exerting some independence. She had been on her own for many years. Independence was something she was forced to learn early in life. She also thought it was one of her better attributes. Clearly that idea was not shared by everyone. "Caya, I have grown to know you and I want you to know that I would give my life for both of you. You have shown great determination to learn our way of life and get to know your mate. You have handled yourself better than anyone could under the circumstances that you have been dealt. You have my respect. I am cautioning you only to keep you both safe."

Caya appreciated Seth's honesty and concern. "How dangerous will this trip be for him?" Seth let out a deep breath. "It is extremely dangerous. However, Nick is the right person to handle this and he can definitely hold his own. I have seen him in action many times in our lifetime. My concern this time is that it is not just the pack he is protecting, but a mate as well." Caya looked at a few pine cones on the ground and gently kicked them around as if she were passing the ball in soccer practice. Seth kept his eyes on her, awaiting her response. When she lifted her head, he could tell by her countenance that whether she realized it or not her feelings ran very deep for her mate. Worry lines had formed in the center of her forehead like ruts in the dirt road leading to the lake after some of the guys had taken their trucks to the lake after a big rain.

She looked him in the eye and said, "I will allow Will to dictate my every move. I will stay within this compound and not put myself in any danger. I will also do my best to convince Nick of all of this as well." Seth smiled. "Poor Will. I feel sorry for him already. I failed to mention that I was thinking of him too when I told you to mind your p's and q's. Don't worry. I will bring our Alpha back to you and the pack safe and thank you for listening and not lashing out at me because I was telling you how to act. I know that was hard for you." Caya laughed, "More than you will ever know dude." He wrapped his big burly arm around her and led her to the house. Seth stopped at the front door and held it open for her. Caya stopped and turned to him and replied, "Promise me." Seth looked confused. Caya continued, "Promise you will take care of him. If I am going to have to bite my tongue all week, you better keep your promise to bring him home safe." Seth gave her a big grin and said, "I promise."

As they entered the living room, she saw the guys huddled around the television. She would never understand how these huge, mostly grown men could sit around a big screen and play

Halo on the Playstation or sit at a computer and play Minecraft. They were headed to breach another werewolf pack and here they were playing games. Seth went to the office as Nick was exiting it. He approached Caya and gave her a weary smile. He was trying to put on a good show for her, but she could see the concern and weariness that he was feeling.

Nick wrapped his arm around her shoulders and led her back to the porch. He motioned for her to sit on the first step where he joined her. "What did you make Seth promise you?" She looked away and pretended to be interested in the daffodils growing alongside the porch. She did not want to rat Seth out; therefore she had no clue how to respond. Nick could see that she was struggling to give a response. He let her squirm for a few more seconds and then asked, "Did he talk to you about our trip?"

Caya recalled she had said she would try to make Nick believe she would be a good girl while he was gone so she might as well spit it out. "Well, yes. I assured Seth and I am assuring you that I will listen to Will and will not invoke my independence while you are gone. I will allow him to shadow me and I will not leave this pri… I mean sanctuary while you are away." Nick looked down at his clasped hands. Caya had not really noticed how strong they were. Most men's hands are large, but his hands had sinews that were very visible to her untrained eye. Then, she started wondering what he would have to do with those strong hands while he was away. Nick moved his fingers unlacing them and grabbing her hand. He could tell that she was trembling when he took her hand. He wasn't sure whether she was scared of him or for him. He took his other hand and placed a finger under her chin and turned her head to face him. "I never want you to feel that you are in a prison here. I want this to be your home. Also, and this is a direct order from your mate, I want you to always be you. Will is learning what that means and he is up for the challenge. With that being said, I never want you to knowingly put yourself in danger. While I am away, I want you to carry on with the routine you have established and allow Will to shadow you. If you can manage that, then when I return we may let you off your leash."

Caya and Nick couldn't help but laugh at that last statement. Nick continued, "I am not sure what Seth said to you, but don't worry about me. I am taking my best men with me and we are going to garner a pact with this pack and I will return home as soon as possible. I am not sure how this separation is going to affect us, but you can rely on my mom and Felicia to help you through it." Caya laid her head on Nick's shoulder. As they watched the moon rise in the sky, she said, "I will and I will. I think worrying when you are away is part of a mate's job and you know I take my roll seriously." He let out a long breath, "That I do." As they sat there viewing the high, thin clouds shroud the moon, Caya could feel something stir within her. It was as if she and her wolf knew this separation was not going to be easy.

Chapter 11

Caya awoke to the sun beaming in through her bedroom window. She sat up with a start. How could she have slept so late? Despite the impending departure, she had slept like a log, well almost. Logs don't typically toss and turn throughout the night. Ok, maybe that is why she slept late. She may not have slept as well as she thought she had. As she arose and sauntered over to the dresser and closet to grab clothes for the day, she was keenly aware that something was missing. She felt like something was missing. As she dressed, she tried to pinpoint why she felt so different. She felt as if part of her soul was missing. That is when she realized that she couldn't feel Nick's presence within her.

She had grown accustomed to feeling him with her even when he was not physically with her. She raced out the door and no one was about the house which was foreign to her because bustle in the house was the usual morning ritual. She headed for the kitchen. When she entered, she looked at the head of the table. He was not there. Halina was sitting at the table with a cup of coffee in her hand. She could see the panic creep into Caya as she looked about the room. Halina stood, "They left earlier. He didn't want to wake you. Sit down and I will get your breakfast." Caya walked to the head of the table and sat. Shock and disbelief were written all over her face. "He left without saying good…goodbye?"

Halina placed a plate of blueberry pancakes in front of the girl as she just stared at the table as if it could conjure up her mate. "He didn't want to wake you. He said for you to call him as soon as you were up. Would you like me to go get your phone while you eat?" Caya continued to stare at the table as she responded, "I don't feel hungry at the moment. Where is Will?" Will sauntered into the kitchen. "You raced right past me. I was sitting in the living room." Will sat at the table and gave a worried look to Halina. They both looked at Caya who was still staring at the table. She finally lifted her head and looked at Will. "I need to alter our schedule. I feel like I need some time to myself. Could we move my lessons to this evening?" pleaded Caya. Will looked at Halina and then back at Caya before he responded. "If that is what you want to do, but don't think you get a vacation this week." Caya looked back to the table. "No, I will be ready for my lessons later. I think I will go get a shower. Thank you for the breakfast. I will eat it later for lunch." She stood and left the table and its occupants who were more than a little concerned about her.

She went back to her room, picked up her phone from the nightstand by the bed. She went to the bathroom and closed the door. She placed her back against the door and slid to the floor. She looked at her phone for several minutes before scrolling in her address book to find Nick's phone number. The highlighted number stared back at her and after several more minutes she pressed the call button. She couldn't tell if Nick's uplifting, "Good morning sleepy head," was forced or not. She simply responded herself with, "Good morning to you too." The seconds ticked by in silence before he went into defensive mode. "I didn't want to wake you this morning. I thought you might have had a fitful night. I didn't want to leave without saying goodbye, but I just didn't have the heart to wake you."

Caya wanted to lash out and say, "*You are such a coward to be an Alpha. You were just afraid to say goodbye to me.*" She bit her tongue for the first time this week. She restrained her tone and said, "I understand. Thanks for thinking of me. (Bite tongue again) Have you arrived to your destination?" Nick sounded tired when he replied, "No. We have just started up the mountain. It will take another hour or so to get to the Mount Rainier estate." Caya's cognizance set in and she said, "Do you have me on the hands-free set where Seth can hear me?" Seth spoke up, "I can hear you Caya." She responded with "Oh." She heard rumbling and something falling and a word slip and then Nick's voice, "I have the phone and it is just you and I. Are you ok?" Before responding to his question, she remembered her conversation with Seth, where she promised to behave and not give Nick any reasons to worry. "Yes, I am fine. I just thought I would see you before you left." Nick apologized once again for not waking her.

Caya could hear Nick take in a deep breath when she asked, "Nick, do you feel different?" She had to know if he was feeling the same abyss that she was feeling. He responded with, "Do you mean do I feel like part of me has been ripped out? The answer is yes." Caya could feel the coolness of the tile floor seeping through her thick jeans. A tear started to escape from her left eye and roll down her cheek. When Caya didn't respond to Nick, he said, "It is ok. We will get through this. You can lean on my mom and I have Seth." Caya held the sob back from her voice. "I shouldn't have asked." Nick reprimanded her. "We need to talk about these things. This is new for me as well. I want to know what you are feeling. I should not have left like I did. I just couldn't see you before I left or I may have stayed."

There it was; the truth as to why he left like he did. Caya had to respond to him or he would think she was upset. "I will be ok. I understand why you left the way you did. I just panicked this morning when I couldn't feel your presence." Nick whispered, "Me too." Caya appreciated the fact that Nick was not too much of a man or wolf to admit that to her. Caya told Nick she had to start her day. He told her he would try to call every day, but he wasn't sure what time he would be able to call. The last thing she said to him was "be safe," and his response was "always." After Caya ended the call, she began to weep. After her pity party was over, she couldn't believe she was acting like such a whipped puppy. She had to get herself together and not mope for the whole week. Things were what they were and she had to get on with life. *A week is not very long. I will keep myself busy and I won't even miss him. I shouldn't miss him anyway. We hardly know each other.* Deep down she knew that was not true. They were making more and more of a connection with each passing day.

Caya walked through the day as if she was part of the Zombie Apocalypse. When she finally made it to the gym to work with Will he had already been working up a sweat with the weight machine. She couldn't help notice his broad shoulders as he sat looking at himself in the wall mirror. She noticed the strain of his muscles as the weights lifted little by little behind his back. She was looking at Will, but picturing Nick's face when she viewed Will's face in the mirror. She tried to shake off the image and act normal.

Will smiled at her as she came closer and she smiled back at his image in the mirror. He dropped the weights, stood and turned to face her. Wiping the sweat from his face, he asked, "Are you ready or do you want to walk on the treadmill first?" She sauntered over to the treadmill. "I will walk while you finish your workout." Once they were on the mat, it was all business. Although Will could tell she wasn't giving 100 percent, he was surprised that she was working as hard as she was considering her current emotional state.

They were finishing up with headlocks when Felicia came into the gym. She waited patiently for instructor and student to finish. Caya walked off the mats and headed toward Felicia. "What are you doing out here? Nick says you are allergic to exercise." Felicia furrowed her brow. "My brother has always been a pain in the butt and apparently that continues when he is out of town." They went outside and sat on a black, iron bench that appeared to have been handmade and welded sporting a wolf that adorned the entire iron backrest.

"Caya, Puyallup High School needs a substitute teacher tomorrow to cover an English class. We were wondering if you would be interested." Caya was taken by surprise. Felicia couldn't quite make out if she was more shocked or overjoyed by the prospect. "I think that is just the distraction that I need. Yes, I would love to go teach tomorrow." Caya went to bed that night with something to look forward to for the next day. This was the key to getting through the week. She just had to remind herself that Nick had many of the pack members with him and he knew what he was doing. She knew if she could stay busy, the time would fly right by, at least she hoped that was the case.

Chapter 12

When Nick pulled his truck into a parking lot outside the Mount Rainier estate, the place was all a bustle. People were walking from building to building. No one was there to greet them as he thought it best not to announce his planned visit. Although the recently deceased Alpha, had met him at his commune, Nick had never been invited to visit the Mount Rainier pack. The buildings were no more than rustic cabins. The ones he could see seemed to be in good repair, but he could tell this commune was not recently settled. He also could tell they were routed in deep tradition and were not looking to modernize. Well, at least this was his initial impression upon arrival. The Puyallup guys parked and began to disembark from their vehicles. Nick and Seth made their way toward the larger of the buildings, which Nick assumed would be a communal building. The rest of his entourage followed close, trusting their Alpha's lead.

Before they reached the building, the door opened and a big, burly guy appeared. His brows gathered into a point toward his nose and it appeared his long, black hair would stand on end if it were not being held in a ponytail. "It is common courtesy for one pack to ask permission of the home pack for a visit." Nick stopped short, as did the other men with him. "I felt that under your current circumstances I should not announce this visit. We are sorry to hear of the loss your Alpha and I am here to make sure there will be a smooth transition of power. With whom am I speaking?" "Well, well, well, it seems that you may be encroaching on our territory. I am sure you would like to see a transition of power straight into your hands. Yes, I recognize you Nick Wilhelm of the Puyallup pack. I see your parents saw that you had a proper education based on the phrasing of your words. I hope you govern as well as you talk, or are you all talk?"

Seth moved toward the rival, but Nick placed a hand in front of his chest to keep him in place. "We may not be as civilized as you," the burly man replied while swiping an arm around indicating their rustic commune. "However, we have our bylaws and plenty of man power to make sure things run smoothly. By the way, you are talking to Riker, the Beta of this pack."

Nick noticed Riker's hands curl into fists. "It is nice to meet you Riker. I am afraid you know more about me than I know about you, which puts me at a disadvantage." Riker smiled as he said, "That is not all that puts you at a disadvantage." With just one look from Nick, Seth received his order to stay.

Nick knew Seth would like to get his hands on Riker, but he would have to stand in line. Nick had first dibs on this guy. "Well, Riker, you may not be happy to see us, but we have driven a while for this visit and your bylaws dictate that you are to provide us shelter as long as we are not being aggressive." Nick's friendly smile was not lost on Riker, but he didn't feel very welcoming to this group of interlopers. However, he did invite them into the building for more constructive conversation.

Nick realized very quickly that Riker was going to be a formidable opponent. He was very keen and knew exactly why Nick had come to Mount Rainier and it was not for the scenery.

Riker did act the good host and had the females bring the men food for which Nick was grateful as his men were famished. This building was used for communal eating. It was lined with long folding tables and chairs. The females must have some influence here as the tables held tablecloths and fall centerpieces. In addition, there were rustic pictures of wildlife and mountain scenery framed in painted barn wood adorning the walls.

As the men ate, Riker eyed them suspiciously. Once Nick was finished eating Riker called some men over to escort the visitors to their sleeping quarters and he and Nick headed to another building centered in the middle of the compound. This building, although rustic looking, seemed to have a little more character with its shrubbery along the front, painted shutters of a red hue, and the same red enveloped the front door. It apparently housed a basement as there were several steps that led up to the front porch.

The rivals entered the home which reflected a lived in aura. They headed to an office off to the right of the home. The office must have belonged to the late Alpha based on all of the paperwork strewn from one end of the room to the other and the pictures of various youngsters framing the walls. Nick felt a kinship with this former leader. Nick could tell from the photos that he loved his pack. Riker motioned Nick to take a seat in front of the desk as he spoke first, "Well, Nick, let's just get to business shall we? You are here to make a claim on my pack." Nick did not mince words. "Yes, I am. However, if I can stay a few days and you convince me that this pack will fare better with you as their Alpha I will have no need to lay claim to your pack. Our packs can continue to live in harmony in this region of Washington State." Riker steepled his fingers as he glared at Nick. Riker, in turn, knew that Nick was going to be a formidable opponent. He needed to wait a little while to see how he wanted this to play out, even if it riled his fur. So let the show begin.

Chapter 13

Caya awoke with the same void she had felt yesterday, but she did look forward to being in an educational environment once again. She had to admit that she really missed teaching. She wondered how opposed Nick would be to allowing her to continue in her chosen profession. She dressed quickly and made her way to the kitchen. Halina had her breakfast made and a lunch prepared for later. Felicia and Will accompanied Caya to Puyallup High. The school looked rather new. Felicia explained that the former building had been built when they used asbestos and had to be torn down and disposed of carefully. The new building had only been occupied for two years. The halls were all a flutter with teenage bodies moving like a herd of cattle through the hallway. Teachers made quick work of corralling the herd into the rooms. The principal met Caya just outside the office. She was very welcoming and wished Caya a good day.

Felicia knew which room Caya would occupy so she led the way. When she entered the classroom, Caya felt at home among the bookshelves that housed many American classics. She appreciated the posters of all of the well-known authors, of those same classics, that adorned the walls. Felicia whispered her well wishes into Caya's ear and then made a fast retreat. Caya could feel how uncomfortable Felicia felt in this atmosphere. Will, however, continued to be her shadow as was his job. He found a chair in the corner at the front of the room and made himself comfortable. Caya looked out among the sea of students and while her countenance showed a glowing smile the students seemed to look at she and Will with awe. Even though she knew nothing of these students, she had felt more at home here than she had in months.

The students had settled into their seats and continued to look at Caya as if she were crazy. She finally decided to introduce herself to them. "I am Miss Braswell. I will be your teacher today and I am looking forward to getting to know you. Although, I am new to this area, I am not new to teaching. I am an English teacher and I must warn you that my love for books is contagious so don't get too worried if you leave here wanting to go straight to the library to procure some for yourself. I see that we are supposed to work on some grammar exercises out of the textbook today. I am sure that your teacher had no idea that I would be filling in for her today, so I am going to alter the lesson a bit. I hope you don't mind." Caya was pleased by the laughing because that was an indication that they were warming toward her.

One young man with short blonde hair raised his hand. At Caya's acknowledgement, he asked, "Miss Braswell there is no need to introduce yourself. Only the dead in the cemetery would not know who you were. Everybody in Puyallup and probably across the werewolf nation, know your story. Is it true that you were not born a werewolf and you were just turned into one?" Caya's face turned a little pink and she turned to Will for help. A lot of help he was. He just sat in his chair and shrugged his shoulders. Caya decided if everyone knew her story then she might as well fess up so she affirmed this to be the case. The boy smiled and said, "Well, you will not have trouble from us Miss Braswell. We are happy our Alpha has found his mate and we are happy that you could join us today." Caya considered the ice broken so she explained the lesson for the day.

Caya instructed the students to tell her about the Puyallup werewolf way of life. They could use the vehicle of their choice. They could write poetry, narratives, or exposition. She explained that this would enhance their writing experience and she would learn more about her new way of life. The students seemed to like the idea that this was not just any assignment, but rather a way to educate the teacher on a topic with which she was just becoming acquainted. All three classes were happy with the assignment for the day. Caya just hoped their regular teacher didn't mind. Many of the students chose to write expository papers explaining their way of life. The more artsy students included illustrations with their prose.

By the end of the day, Caya was exhausted, but also elated. Felicia picked Caya and Will up after school. Felicia could tell by the smile on Caya's face that she had succeeded in helping Caya forget about Nick for a little while at least. Caya was all Chatty Cathy when she eased into the car. She couldn't wait to tell Felicia about her day and Felicia couldn't wait to hear.

When they arrived home, Caya noticed she had missed a call from Nick. She felt very guilty for not having taken that call. She was not sure when he would be able to call again. She hoped he would be excited when she told him what she had been up to today. She was like a kid in a candy store. She couldn't wait to speak to him, but she didn't want to call and interrupt him if he was in a business meeting. She resigned herself to wait for his next call.

Chapter 14

Nick and Seth shared a room and the other guys shared three other rooms in the same cabin. The cabin was neat and clean, but he could tell that this cabin had not been occupied in some time. When they had arrived, males and females of the hosting pack brought necessities into the cabin that would be needed for the week. Before leaving the cabin, Nick gave his pack strict orders to stay inside until he returned. He was very concerned about everyone's safety while they were here. It was one thing to risk his own life, but he was risking many of his pack by bringing them here, but he knew before they left he would need their help.

He and Seth made their way to Riker's cabin early of the morning before too much hustle and bustle started the day. Riker was in his office when the pair arrived. For this meeting the Mount Rainier Beta was not alone. There was another Mount Rainier pack member in the room and Nick could hear the raised voices. Nick could make out Riker's commanding voice, "I am the rightful leader next in the succession. I can lead this pack without interference from the Puyallup pack!" The other voice was husky, but not as commanding as Riker's voice, "What are you going to do about them?" "What do you think I am going to do with them? I am going to send them back home with their tails between their legs!" Nick looked at Seth and Seth gave Nick the *I am with you* look.

Nick felt it was time to make his presence known so he entered the house and stepped into the doorway of the office where Riker sat on the edge of his desk red faced. Nick recognized anger and there was nothing more dangerous than a power hungry werewolf who thinks you are intruding on his terrain.

Nick pierced the Beta with his gaze and said, "Riker I don't think your remarks are a great show for your ability to lead this group of wolves. You should also know that I do not plan on going home with my tail between my legs." The corner of Riker's mouth rose a little at his own little joke. "I would have been disappointed if you had." He looked to his comrade and with his head motioned for him to leave the room. Nick noticed immediately that the guy had no hesitation, which indicated Riker was use to giving orders and this member of the pack was use to accepting them.

Nick took a seat in front of his adversary, who remained perched on the corner of the desk. They were so close in proximity that their knees almost touched. Nick wasted no time getting to business. "As Beta of the pack, you would be in succession for the role of Alpha if your pack backed you. Have you had anyone oppose you since your Alpha has passed?" Nick could have seen the hackles rise on Riker's neck if the Beta were in wolf form. "There have been none to speak of. You are the only challenger at the moment. What claim do you think you have on this pack?"

Nick looked straight back into the eyes of his nemesis and replied, "Since I have been an Alpha for several years now, my experience in the role speaks for itself. Likewise, it is my duty as Alpha to grow my pack and keep it safe. I cannot chance leaving this pack to inept governance which could bring danger to this pack as well as mine." Riker rose from the desk and walked over to the window where he gazed at the morning sun. After a minute, he spoke, "I may never have been Alpha, but I do know my people and I am ready to lead." Nick rose from the chair and made his way to the door. Before exiting, he turned half a turn and exclaimed, "We will see." Nick and Seth left Riker to his thoughts and went back to the cabin in which they inhabited. Seth asked Nick, "Do you think he will have to be removed?" Nick shook his head. "That remains to be seen. We only have a few days to figure it out." His pack was restless so he went with them further into the woods so they could change forms and take a run. He was going to accompany them for fear that the Mount Rainier pack may jump his men. He would not leave them alone to fight his battle.

When he returned to the cabin, the guys decided to watch television or read. He went to his room and called Caya. She had not answered his call earlier in the morning. He couldn't imagine why she would not be eager to speak to him. When they had spoken yesterday, she seemed very down. He hoped that his mother was a comfort to her while he was away. She would be able to anticipate Caya's every need being of the female and former Alpha mate persuasion.

Caya had been on the phone with Rayna. She couldn't wait once she was home to call her best friend to tell her about her day at Puyallup High. Rayna was excited to hear from Caya, whom she missed terribly. Rayna was able to detect a renewed happiness in her friend that she had not heard in her voice since she had moved in with Nick. Rayna didn't think Caya was unhappy, but she did detect that she seemed unsettled. She wished Caya would open up to her and explain what was going on in her newly chartered life. It was so unlike Caya to abandon her responsibilities at school and to her best friend and her boyfriend and run off to people she did not know. Rayna wanted to trust her and give her space, but she also felt that she was letting her down by not insisting on more of an explanation. Caya probably had had a nervous breakdown and lost her ever loving mind. The change in Caya's voice relieved Rayna's concern. She listened to Caya's whole rendition of the day as if she were watching it unfold on the big screen. Rayna missed her bestie and wished they could see more of each other. A face-to-face meeting may allay some of Rayna's concern for her friend.

Caya had really missed her friend and was so relieved when she answered the phone and was able to give the account of her day. It felt like old times when they shared an apartment as well as all of their ups and downs in life. Caya wished she could share with Rayna more about her current life, her insecurities, her new found love interest, her new way of life. She wanted to divulge everything to her honorary sister.

Caya had no siblings and when her parents died her friend was by her side and they were inseparable up until werewolf Ville. It was so good to hear her voice. Before they finished their conversation, they had decided to meet for a shopping rendezvous the next day. She heard her phone beep and as she pulled the phone from her ear and looked at the caller id on the screen immediately felt guilty when she noticed Nick's number displayed. She had promised to stay on the estate while he was away. Maybe she could talk Will into allowing her to meet Rayna if she allowed him to stick to her like glue during the whole excursion. Caya explained to Rayna that she had another call coming in and she would see her at their favorite restaurant for lunch and shopping tomorrow.

Caya's voice betrayed her excitement when she said, "Hello!" "You sound way too excited to have been moping around the house all day. You didn't answer when I called this morning. Should I have called Will first to hear his version of how you spent your day?" Caya could feel her excitement relent to the anger that was surfacing. "You do not expect me to sit around the house and pine for you all week do you, Nick Wilhelm? If so, you better think again. I lived many years without you in my life and I am not so far gone that I can't be without you for one week."

This was not how Nick expected this conversation with Caya to go. He was somewhat taken aback by her anger. He didn't realize that he had said anything wrong. He was just teasing her. "Whoa, whoa, whoa. I was just teasing Caya. There is no need to get all upset. I am happy you are not at home pining for me. I think." Caya calmed a little. It was ok for her to tease and aggravate Nick, but apparently she could dish it out, but she couldn't take it.

"You might want to call Will and get his version of my day. I think I would even like to hear it. Actually, I have had a superb day. I taught English at Puyallup High School today. I enjoyed every minute of it. The students seemed to respond well to me and I felt right at home with them. They were a little taken aback when I entered the room. Did you know that they already knew who I was? They couldn't believe I was there to teach them. They were very well behaved, but I imagine that my relationship to you had something to do with that. I had them writing about their way of life. I hope to get some insight into this way of life through their teenage eyes. Knowing teenagers the way I do, some of it may need to be censored."

Nick jumped into the conversation when Caya took a breath. "Slow down and take a few breaths. I am not sure enough oxygen is getting to your brain. I am really glad that you had such an invigorating day, but I can't believe that you wanted to go to the school to teach. Are you that bored? Did you take Will with you?" Caya paused before giving a response. "Yes, I took Will. I told you that I would let him shadow me. Don't worry. I was perfectly safe. I told Seth I would stay on the estate while you were gone and I think that the school can be considered part of the estate since it is adjacent to it and many of the young pack members attend there. Please don't be mad. I really miss teaching and I was feeling lost because of this void that I feel due to your absence. This is just what I needed to keep me from free falling into an abyss. Can't you just be happy for me Nick?"

Nick wasted no time in answering her. "Of course I want to join in your excitement. I guess I thought you would take on different interests now. I am glad you had a great day." Caya didn't know whether she should accept his response or not, "take on new interests?" She let it slide for now, but this was a conversation for another time, a time when they were not separated by many miles and communicating through a cell phone. She decided that she would take the shopping issue up with Will and not mention it to Nick for the moment.

Caya decided it was best to change topics to how Nick spent his day. Nick was not very forthcoming with information about what was going on at Mount Rainier. He had just said that things were progressing as he had expected and he was not enjoying himself half as much as she seemed to be enjoying herself. Caya decided to not take this as another dig from Nick. She refused to let her uplifted spirit be drowned by this phone call. They continued to chat about the weather and other mundane topics for a few more minutes before Nick said he had to go eat dinner. They said their goodbyes and Caya ended the conversation by reminding him to stay safe to which he replied, "Always."

Caya pleaded her case to Will that night concerning the shopping trip scheduled for the following day. He was not keen on the idea, to put it bluntly. She knew he felt it was easier to keep her safe if she were within the compound. However, she really needed to spend time with her friend Rayna. Caya needed the companionship and Rayna needed to know that Caya had not totally abandoned her. Will might be her instructor and protector, but he had a soft spot for Caya and he didn't want to deny her anything. He saw how she struggled day-to-day with her new life and although he couldn't totally comprehend her situation he did know if the tables were turned he didn't think he would be handling it as well as she seemed to be handling it. He finally conceded and Caya put him in a bear hug he would not soon forget.

Caya insisted on driving her new Charger and Will didn't seem to mind. He was up for a ride in a sports car. All of the guys drove trucks and he kind of felt a little wild at the thought of a ride in her car. He just wished he were driving. As they headed out of the house to the car, Caya literally ran into James' grandpa. "Oh, sorry grandpa, what are you doing here?" Grandpa had caught her by the shoulders to keep her from tumbling to the porch. Once she was sure-footed again he replied, "I am here to keep an eye on things. You know when the cat is away the mice will play." Caya giggled, "Oh grandpa!" "Where are you and Will headed today, Caya?" "We are going to meet my friend Rayna for a day of shopping." Grandpa gave her a hug and whispered in her ear, "I am glad to see that smile back on your face. Be careful and don't stray from Will." Caya was hugging him back.

When she and James were dating, she had always enjoyed being around his grandpa. He apparently knew she was not a werewolf then and had accepted her anyway. His was the only familiar face in a sea of strangers when she first came to Puyallup. He didn't make her feel uncomfortable since she was no longer just human Caya Braswell, but now a mate to a different wolf. "I promise to be careful. Thanks grandpa." With that she was off to deploy her new toy. Although it had been great to see grandpa again, it seemed strange to Caya that he was hanging around the house. He usually kept to himself or he had since she came into the picture. I guess when Nick was away it was all hands on deck, including grandpa.

When Caya and Rayna reached each other, they were twirling around giggling like two teenage girlfriends. They ate Mexican and then started their shopping spree. Caya was always cognizant of where Will was in relation to her. She felt so free, with the exception of having a shadow, her time with Rayna felt like old times. Rayna had asked about Nick's whereabouts and why Will was hanging around. Caya let the question slide. To his credit, he had tried to keep some distance as not to be privy to their conversation and grant them some privacy. However, he never let Caya out of his sight.

Once they had had their fill of shopping, Rayna headed back to her apartment. She was meeting her boyfriend, Lars, there and they were going out to dinner and to a movie. Caya told Will she needed to make a pit stop by the ladies room. There was one located in the outside outlet mall near where she was parked. She gave Will the keys to the Charger and told him he could wait for her at the car. He gave her the *oh no you don't* look and fell in line behind her. She turned abruptly and face planted into his chest. "Are you going to follow me into the restroom? Will, I think I am capable of going to the restroom without a bodyguard." Will's face turned deep red. Caya wasn't sure if it was from embarrassment or anger.

Once they had separated, he found his voice, "Of course I know you do not need my assistance to **use** the restroom, but anything can happen between the restroom and your car. "Really, Will, I will be fine. It is what maybe fifty yards. You will only lose sight of me when I round one store to get to the restroom. I will watch all around me. You must trust you have trained me well. If I need you, I will yell." Against his better judgement, he looked at his dusty cowboy boots and said, "Ok. I guess there will be no harm in your going that far without me breathing down your neck." Caya stood on her tiptoes and kissed the top of his head while he still inspected his boots. "Thanks Will!" With that, she was gone. He didn't panic until she had not returned in twenty minutes.

Caya had entered the restroom, taken care of business, washed her hands and was headed out of the restroom when an arm snaked around her waist and a hand covered her mouth. She immediately thought the kidnapper to be Will trying to teach her a lesson about going off on her own. Therefore, she allowed her training to lead her. As if they were in the gym, on the mats, she elbowed the assailant in the stomach, reached up and brought his head down on her shoulder, and when she heard the crack of his nose, she turned around and placed her knee in his crotch. The kidnapper was groaning in pain and sunk to the mall floor. As she was attacking his crotch, she noticed that this person didn't have Will's hair style, nor was he wearing the tight Under Armor t-shirt that Will had been wearing earlier. Once he was on the floor she pinned him to his back while he still tried to turn into the fetal position to protect his crotch from another onslaught.

She couldn't believe her eyes. She was face to face with James. Before she could say anything to him, another hand grabbed her arm and pulled her up and away from James. She started to retaliate against the second assailant as he said, "It's me Caya." It was Will. He grabbed her and pulled her into his chest while he stared at the damage she had inflicted on her former boyfriend. James got to his feet and ran. He didn't want to have to take on both of them.

Chapter 15

When Nick finished his call to Caya, he was a little perplexed. He wasn't sure how he felt about her teaching again. He knew of her love of books, but they had not really spoken about her teaching career. It had never occurred to him that she missed her career and her students. The more he thought about it the more he was determined that they should speak about her role in the Puyallup pack. He needed to emphasize that as mate to the Alpha of the pack she would have to fulfill certain responsibilities. Those responsibilities may not leave much time for a teaching job. He was having conflicting thoughts. She had sounded so excited when she spoke to him of her day at the school which was a sharp contrast to how she sounded that first day, the day of his departure. That day she didn't have a whole lot to say and had sounded really sad as if she were trying to hold back her crying for his sake. How would they balance her needs with her responsibilities? Well, he had more pressing responsibilities at the moment. Caya's needs would be addressed soon enough, but for now he had to concentrate on his business with the Mount Rainier pack, specifically Riker, before he went rogue.

Nick watched how the members of the host pack interacted with each other and with Riker. He even encouraged his own pack members to interact with the host pack to see how that interaction went. He noticed right away that the Mount Rainier pack interacted what appeared to be normally with each other, but Riker had to approach and initiate conversation with his own pack members, with the exception of his right-hand man. They didn't initiate conversation with Riker. When members of the Puyallup pack tried to initiate conversation with members of the Mount Rainier pack, the host pack was very reluctant to engage in conversation. Nick decided to watch for today and then try to socialize tomorrow.

Just like Riker, these wolves knew why Nick and his entourage were here and they were not a trusting group. Riker tried to ignore Nick, but as Riker walked by, Nick left his chair and walked up to him. "Riker, where is the deceased Alpha's mate? Does she still live within the pack?" Riker appeared to be irritated by the questions. "She does. She may or may not give you an audience. Why are you interested in her? I hear you already have your own mate, a virgin one at that. If you are looking to trade her in, I might be interested." Now, Nick was invading Riker's personal space. They were eye to eye. It was Seth's turn to step in and put a hand on Nick's shoulder and pull him back. With clenched teeth, Nick expounded, "Apparently, you have yet to find your own mate so you would like to have mine. From what I see right now, you aren't man enough for her." That was all it took for Riker to reach Nick's personal space and blows started flying. Pack members from both camps started circling the two adversaries ready to jump in if anyone from the opposing pack interfered. Several punches had been thrown and both opponents were bleeding from the face before a female voice spoke with authority, "Enough of this boyish behavior. One of you is an Alpha and the other wishes to be. Neither of you is acting like a leader at the moment. Enough!"

Nick was now introduced to the former Alpha's widow. She didn't introduce herself and apparently there was no reason for Nick to introduce himself as she seemed to already know about him. She maneuvered her head to indicate to Nick that he should go to the empty table to her right and his left, as they were facing one another. Once she and Nick sat down, she started the conversation. "Ok Nick. I understand that you are here to lay claim to the Mount Rainier pack. My mate would have respected your initiative. Riker, on the other hand, will most likely resent it. Riker has been a good Beta to my mate, but I am not sure he has the temperament to be Alpha. He is loyal to those he respects. I am not sure that respect is transferred to you."

Nick respected this woman's leadership and concern for her pack. He also respected the fact that she was willing to speak about her concern of Riker's leadership abilities. "It seems you know me, but I don't know you," replied Nick. This woman who appeared to be in her late thirties just gave a sly smile. "It is my business as an Alpha's mate to know about the other packs in the vicinity of home. My role as a leader of this pack died with the death of my mate. Of course the pack members will still take care of me, but I will never take on another mate so Riker just looks down on me. I am much too old for him and definitely not submissive enough for him."

With that comment, Nick smiled. He could relate with that. Fate had joined him with a less than submissive mate as well. However, that was one of her most endearing traits. "I see that you understand that too well," she continued as she chuckled. "Bless you son for you are going to need it. On a more serious note, you should not take Riker lightly. He is determined to take over this pack whether this pack wants his leadership or not. You will be forced to fight for the right to commandeer this pack. I hope you are up for the battle." Nick looked her square in the eye as he spoke, "So you are of the thought that Riker is not the best person to guide this pack?" She merely shook her head. "Well, I guess I will have to prove to this pack that I am the man for this job, even if that means challenging your Beta for the position." The matronly woman just shook her head as she rose to leave. "I wish you the best Alpha. Remember to never let your guard down and watch your back and your mate's too." Nick rose as she rose and he couldn't help notice the confidence she exuded as she walked away from him. He knew that she was someone with whom he should ally himself for this battle.

Chapter 16

Will rushed Caya to the Charger. He placed her in the passenger seat as he eyed everyone in their vicinity. He didn't see James anywhere, but he didn't want to be surprised if he decided to attack as he attacked Caya moments ago. He was proud of the poise she had shown when James had grabbed her. She didn't freeze at the time, but now she seemed to be in a state of shock. She just stared out the windshield as he rounded the car to take the driver's seat. She had not said a word nor moved the whole time they were exiting the parking lot of the mall. He wasn't sure how to get her to talk. Knowing Caya the way he did, she needed time to process what had happened and when she was ready she would speak.

They were almost home and she still had not spoken to him. He chanced a glance in her direction to find that she was still gazing out the windshield. She was breathing normally, not as if she were out of breath like she was when he had ushered her to the car. So he decided he should break the ice. "Caya, are you ok? You don't seem to be bleeding. Are you hurting anywhere?" Caya waited a moment before she turned her head toward Will and issued her response, "No. I am fine and you better not say I told you so." Will looked at her briefly when he said, "That is the last thing you need to hear right now. I am really sorry this happened to you. You don't deserve to be hunted by another wolf as if you are his prey. Unfortunately, in the short time that you have been part of our pack, you have been someone's prey twice. I know you resent me having to follow you around all of the time, but I hope that these incidents prove to you the need for my presence and the need for you to learn to defend yourself. I was very proud of how you handled the situation and Nick will be as well."

At that remark, Caya became responsive. "Will, you can't tell Nick. Please. He will never let me leave the house. I really will be a prisoner." Will felt sorry for her when he saw her panic stricken face. No wolf wants to be caged. The thought of Caya being caged was in stark contrast to the free spirit he saw all day today when she was out in her element with someone she loved, having the time of her life. Will and Caya did not speak for the remainder of their drive home.

When they pulled in front of the house, Will put the Charger in park and turned the key to the off position. He then turned his body so that he was face to face with his protegé. "You know that he is my Alpha and you are his mate. He entrusts your safety and education to me. You know that means that he holds me in high regard. I have to give him updates on your progress as well as any safety concerns that I may see that threaten you. When we enter this house, I will call him and make my report about where we went today and what danger you encountered. However, I will also emphasize how you took control of the situation and handled the threat without any interference from me. Nick knows to expect these dangerous situations. That is why he has had me training you. I have the highest regard for Nick and I think you should give him credit for his decisiveness as our pack leader. He will handle the news of this threat better than you may think, but, Caya, you need to know that although I will always protect you, I will also always obey and respect my Alpha."

Caya merely looked at her hands and nodded in consent before exiting the vehicle. She left Will to make his report and she took refuge in her library upstairs. Once she entered the room and found sanctuary in her comfy wing back chair, emotion overtook her and she began to sob and shake uncontrollably. Images of what she had just encountered came playing through her mind. *What was James thinking? Why did he try to kidnap me? I thought we finally had an understanding. Did Nick suspect this would happen? Is that why he was so adamant that I learn to defend myself and have a bodyguard? How many more encounters of this magnitude will I have to face? Will I freeze the next time? I don't even want to think about how Nick will react to what happened. Will asked me to trust that Nick would handle this better than I think he will. Something tells me I might be right this time and Will may be too optimistic.*

Will went to his room to make his phone call to Nick. He was not looking forward to this conversation. He really did believe what he had told Caya about Nick being fair in his decision making. He had known all along that there would come a day when he would have to make a report like this to his Alpha, but more importantly to Caya's mate. He knew that he was ready to rip James' limbs apart. He couldn't imagine what Nick would want to do to him. Nick answered on the first ring. "Will, are you both ok?" Will was not surprised by the direct question. Nick would know that Will would only call him if there was a problem. He also knew that Nick was expecting situations to arise while he was away. That is why he was reluctant to leave.

"We are fine and she did what she needed to do to escape." Nick made no response as he closed his eyes and pinched the bridge of his nose. He knew this day would come, but he hoped it wouldn't arrive so soon. "Give me the play by play." Will began to explain to his Alpha about the shopping trip and how he had let Caya go to the ladies room without being shadowed by him. He apologized for his lapse in judgement, but told Nick that he went in search of her as soon as he became concerned. He also explained how Caya had convinced him to stay behind and that he felt she had a valid point about needing to trust her training. Will hoped Nick agreed. He also described the scene on which he arrived and the condition in which he found James.

Nick was relieved that she had neutralized the situation and had not panicked to the point that she could not defend herself. He thanked Will for taking care of her and agreed that it was time for Caya to be allowed to take a roll in her safety. He also hoped that this incident would open her eyes to how serious he had been about the threats that surround her. Unfortunately, this was only one of them. Nick was not oblivious to the many others that were out there and now he probably could add his buddy, Riker to that list of threats against his mate. When their conversation ended, Nick took a deep breath before pressing the speed dial number on his cell phone to call the love of his life, all while thanking God for her not being injured in this attack or worse kidnapped by a jealous ex-boyfriend that just happened to be a wolf from another pack.

Caya answered the call with reluctance. Her "Hello," was very soft this time, not nearly as exuberant as their last conversation. Nick simply asked, "How are you?" Caya wasn't sure how she should answer. Nick added, "Honestly." She knew she had to answer him honestly. He deserved nothing less. "I am a little shaken up emotionally, but physically I am fine, really." Nick knew how he would respond to other members of his pack, but he wasn't quite sure what he should say to Caya and what he should keep bottled up within himself. He finely decided on praise. "I understand you handled yourself well and were able to neutralize the situation. I am very proud of you."

Caya shot back, "I know you are mad that I asked Will to stay behind and I don't want you to be mad at him. Be mad at me. I need to feel like I am in control of my own safety. I need to see that I can take care of myself if it becomes necessary. There may come a time when Will is out of the picture and I only have myself on which to rely. Today showed me that I can rely on my training if I need to and all of this work was necessary even though I thought it was not. Don't blame Will. He came as soon as I was not back to the car in an appropriate amount of time. He removed me from the threat and saw me safely home. That is all you can ask of him. As for me, I let him shadow me all day with the ladies room being the only exception so if you could cut us some slack I would appreciate it."

Nick couldn't help but smile at her comments. He so missed her and her forthright attitude. "You make good points. I am just thankful you were not injured. I am glad you realize that I was only acting in your best interest when I assigned Will to you and asked him to be your self-defense instructor. I am not mad at either one of you." Caya took the opportunity to ask, "You are not even mad that I went shopping in Tacoma?" Nick answered honestly, "I wish you would have waited until I was home. I don't want to keep you prisoner and I don't want to keep you from your friends, but when I am away that automatically puts you in more danger. That is why I asked you to stay on the estate. I hope today's threat has opened your eyes to some of the danger that you may encounter just because you are my mate. I know you didn't ask for this way of life. However, I hope you will soon see that it is not all bad. There are good aspects of this life as well."

Caya admitted, "It has gotten off to a rocky start." Knowing this to be true, they both snickered into the phone. Nick decided to end the conversation on a light note by asking her how much of his money she left at the mall today. Caya perked up when telling him the good deals she found at each store where she had made purchases. He was glad to hear the strain in her voice leave as she spoke of her new found loot. Before ending the conversation, he did ask her to stay on the estate in light of James still being on the loose and Caya was happy to comply with his request, for a few more days anyway. When Caya ended the call, she was struck by how much better that conversation went than she thought it would. She just knew her mate would be furious enough with her to make her a prisoner in her home until he returned from his trip. She decided that she would stay on the estate until he returned. That was a reasonable compromise. However, this was only day three of seven. Whatever would she do with the rest of her solitary time?

Chapter 17

As Nick walked back to his cabin, he couldn't help but be distracted by the thoughts of what could have happened to his mate if the situation had turned in an unfavorable direction. The leader in him forged the path in their conversation that would only praise her rather than berate her about her decision to leave Will behind. He knew that they were miles apart and this was no time to chastise her. He also knew that she was like a new wolf pup. It would take her time to feel her way through this way of life; mistakes would be made and he just hoped she learned from them. Based on their conversation, Nick felt she now had a better understanding of why he made the decision to place a bodyguard in her company and that he was not just being over protective of her, that his concerns for her safety were real and legitimate.

As he reached the cabin, he noticed a wolf cry piercing the otherwise quiet evening. He looked around and before he could react a wolf the color of midnight pounced on him. Instinct took over and Nick welcomed his own wolf form. The aggressor bit chunks out of the repressor's flank as though he was a piece of steak. Their rolling around on the ground looked more like two pigs in a mud hole rather than two wolves trying to show their dominance. The brown wolf would get the upper hand for a moment and take a few mouthfuls of flesh and then the black wolf would reciprocate. After a few short minutes, other wolves circled the two, watching the melee unfold in front of them. Each pack member was standing at the ready awaiting the opportunity to jump into the fray to help his pack leader. Eventually, the two wrestlers broke apart and stared one another down waiting for the other's next move. The black wolf turned and ran for the woods. The brown wolf just stood his ground and watched him leave, knowing this would not be their last encounter.

It was not lost on Nick how the Mount Rainier pack did not follow their Beta to the woods. Rather, they changed back into their human forms, as did the Puyallup pack. Once skin replaced fur, they retreated to their own cabins. Nick's pack followed him into the cabin and awaited any orders he may wish to utter. However, Nick had no orders for his men. He just wanted to attend to his wounds. His wolf anatomy allowed wounds to heal quickly, but they didn't hurt any less while they were healing. He relished a cold shower to help cool his ire and soothe his bitten flesh. While he was in the shower, he contemplated what his next move would be. He had no doubt his men would follow him through this battle, but it was not as clear if

Riker's men would do the same for him, evidenced by their retreat to their own sanctuaries after the tussle they had witnessed.

Nick awoke during the night to loud thunderstorms and fierce wind. Eventually, the power went out and he was thankful for his keen wolf eyesight. The rain sounded like rocks being dumped on the metal roof. The wind whistled through the trees but the sound was not enough to mask the loud boom that caught Nick's attention. When some of his pack looked out the front window, they witnessed flames being fanned by the wind. When they told Nick what they saw, he began to dress and was followed out into the storm by his companions. Chaos had taken root in the commune. People could be seen running to Riker's cabin. Someone had a water hose and was trying to douse the flames that were surging from the roof. Another person was barking orders for other members of the hosting pack to break the windows and spray water inside the quickly engulfed cabin. The heavy downpour helped stay the fire on the roof, but not before it had wreaked irreparable damage on the deceased Alpha's sanctuary. While everyone worked feverishly to put out the fire, Nick entered the home in search of any occupants that may have not made it out alive.

The smoke was so thick Nick was choking. He couldn't see three feet in front of him. He pulled his t-shirt over his nose, but it did little to keep the smoke from his nostrils. He was forced to his hands and knees still searching for survivors of Mother Nature's wrath. He hoped that the cabin was the only casualty of the lightning strike. Once he had checked the office, the heat from the flames became too intense for him to continue through the rest of the home. He felt a hand grab the back of his leg and start pulling him from the home. Seth continued to pull at his leg until Nick turned around and headed out of the cabin following his best friend. Once outside, they wasted no time filling their lungs with oxygen as the rain continued to pound their overheated bodies. The cool, pelting rain was most welcomed by those trying to keep the fire from reaching other cabins in the vicinity, as well as by the heroes who had entered the inferno in search of Mount Rainier pack members who may have become trapped in their own personal hell on earth.

Before the rain had subsided, the fire was extinguished and no remains were found in the incinerated cabin. There was only a fireplace and front porch stairs left to indicate there had been a building there once. Opposing pack members brought Nick and Seth cups of water to help soothe their smoke irritated throats. Nick endured many pats on the back and accolades for his bravery and compassion for the Mount Rainier pack. Someone asked if anyone had seen Riker. Many of his pack lowered their heads as they replied, "Nowhere to be found." The Puyallup Alpha felt sorry for these wolves that in their time of need were without a leader.

As the sun rose, cleanup began. The Puyallup pack worked alongside the Mount Rainier pack to clear the debris. They all worked in harmony without discord between them. Riker's absence, even with the dawn of a new day, did not go unnoticed. Once the work was complete, everyone convened in the communal building for a feast the women had prepared for the hardworking men. Six older gentlemen were crowded around a table and seemed to be in deep conversation as they ate. The raised voices in the group indicated a heated discussion was taking place among them. The men were still convened when everyone else went to their cabins to relax for the remainder of the evening.

Nick was watching a football game on the television when there was a loud knock at the door. One of his pack members opened the door to a gray haired man who exuded confidence. He entered the cabin and asked if he could speak to Nick in private. Nick stood and indicated with his hand that they should walk outside. Once outside the cabin, the man introduced himself as Waylon, a dear friend of the former Alpha and a member of the pack council. Nick had figured as much as he had watched the men collaborate at dinner. Waylon was not a man of many words. He was there to make an offer and he did not preface the offer with idle conversation. He had been sent by the council to ask Nick to unite the Mount Rainier and Puyallup packs and continue as Alpha. "My pack is very appreciative of your help last night during the fire. We were most impressed by your courage in trying to rescue the one person that would love to take your life. You put your differences aside to rescue him. Riker was not there so you risked your life for nothing. The council is aware that Riker would like to be the Alpha of this pack, but he was not here by our side during our time of trouble. He has never showed compassion to any member of this pack. If that had been your cabin on fire, he would have left you all to fry." After a short pause, he looked Nick in the eye and continued, "Your reputation has preceded you. Many on the council knew and respected your father. We trust you to lead our pack and wish for you to merge this mountain pack with your valley pack."

The men continued to walk around the commune. Although people were still out and about the grounds, they gave the men a wide berth as they walked and talked. Nick stopped abruptly and looked Waylon in the eye. "A great leader must show courage, determination, and compassion. I thank you for your trust in my leadership. I will accept your proposal. I would like to work with the council to appoint someone to govern in my absence." The two men shook hands and went to their perspective cabins for the remainder of the night. They had planned to meet again in the morning at Waylon's cabin where the other council members would join them to hash out the particulars of the governing of the abandoned pack.

Nick and the council spent two days going over the pack bylaws and appointing Waylon to govern in Nick's place when he was in Puyallup. Nick was not certain that things would go smoothly, but he felt that putting someone from the mountain pack in charge would help pave the way and he had decided before coming to Mount Rainier to leave Aaron, Seth's brother and one of his best men here to help see that things were carried out to Nick's specifications. So it was decided that an appointed delegate from each pack would work with the pack council to govern the mountain pack, but Nick would be Alpha of both packs. Since no one had seen Riker, the perspective Alpha of the pack, since his scuffle with Nick the night of the fire, Nick couldn't help but wonder where and when he would show up next because he knew without a doubt he had not seen the last of the black wolf.

Chapter 18

Caya had not heard from Nick the night of the fire. She was worried because he had promised to call her each day and up until now he had stayed true to his promise. It took all the restraint she could muster to keep from dialing his number. Will had indicated that it would not be wise to call him as she had no idea what he might be undertaking at the moment. She wasn't sure what Nick would encounter on his business trip, but just from what she had witnessed since she had joined the pack, she was sure Will meant that he may be in some sort of combat for the ability to lead the perspective pack. She couldn't really fathom what that combat situation would look like, but she did have to remember that the militants were animals.

She was trying to shake off those thoughts as she went in search of Halina, Nick's mother. Halina had asked if she would like to discuss the mating ceremony. With the events of the week, Caya had almost forgotten that Nick had suggested she collaborate with his mother and take care of the plans while he was away. She was very nervous about what the ceremony would entail. She had attended many weddings in her lifetime, but never anything like this. She tried to fantasize what a life as Nick's wife would be. In some respects, he still seemed like a stranger to her, but there was no doubt about how close they had become in the few months that she had been a part of the Puyallup pack. Unfortunately, she still didn't feel that she was one of them, despite their efforts to help her maneuver through this way of life.

She found Halina in the laundry room folding clothes. To look at Halina she was clearly human, but Caya knew that she had another form and it seemed surreal to think that a werewolf would be tending to household chores like laundry. It also seemed odd to think that this sweet mother who welcomed her into her home and who had filled a motherless void in her life was quite capable of killing when necessary. Once Halina spotted Caya, she gave her a warm, welcoming smile. "How are you holding up daughter?" This was the first time that this matron of wisdom had addressed her in such a manner. It took the young woman by surprise. She decided that it was not as odd as she first thought to think of herself in such a way. She welcomed the thought of having a mother to lean on in what had become a tumultuous time in her life.

Caya returned the smile and said, "Well, for someone who was almost kidnapped by one man and abandoned by another I think I am fairing pretty well," and her smile turned into a frown as she thought that her remarks may have offended Nick's mother. To the contrary, Halina just chuckled opting to find the humor in what was said or the situation. Caya was not sure which. "I don't think my son has abandoned you, although it may feel that way at the moment. Have you heard from him today?" Caya merely shook her head to indicate the negative. "Well, he must have found himself in a difficult business meeting. These males will talk until they are blue in the face without making the first decision. Men and their pride may be the downfall of our nation." Caya appreciated Halina describing the situation as a business meeting. It was a little more comforting thinking of her mate in that type of a situation rather than the physical altercations she had been imagining.

"Once you finish your laundry, I wondered if this might be a good time to discuss the mating ceremony." Halina's reaction was what Caya had anticipated. She was all smiles and excitement shown on her face as well as in the detail of her folding. "Of course, do you have questions or do you actually want to start making some plans?" That was the question of the century. Was she ready to take the next step in this relationship? She was of the mind that a couple should date for a couple of years and here she was closing on only six months of knowing Nick. She was still conflicted about her feelings for him and this way of life. She was concerned about how this way of life would alter the way she lived and the dreams she had worked so hard to achieve.

In contrast, she was becoming acutely aware of the danger she was in as long as she was just dating her mate. Completing the mating, would afford her peace of mind of other male wolves trying to convince her to join their ranks or in James' case forcing her to join them. She was clearly still a little raw about that situation.

After her moment of reflection, she responded, "I am sure that I will definitely have questions, but I am ready to move on to the planning stage. After the last few days, I feel that the sooner this bond is created the better Nick and I will be." Halina just nodded in consent. "I know this is new to you and I understand your reluctance to fully turn your life over to my son. I am going to tell you as I would my own daughter that you must know in your heart that Nick is your stronghold. You need to look deep and not just trust the connection you feel with him. Both are important in a marital life. Will this life with him be easy? Don't delude yourself. You have only touched the surface these last few months. You may not find yourself in the same situations, but you will be tested in other ways. However, my dear, from what I have witnessed from you, you are up for the job. If you are unsure, I want you to know from one Alpha's wife to a perspective one that you have what it takes to make this relationship work and to forge your way as a leader in the werewolf world. You just need to believe in yourself, as Nick and I believe in you. Although now you have supernatural strength, it is your inner strength that draws us to you."

Caya was so thankful for this conversation. Her future mother-in-law had thrown her the very life preserver she needed in her mind of uncertainty. "Let us proceed with the planning then and, Halina, could we make it as soon as possible?" Her adopted mother walked over and embraced the young woman as Caya felt little wet droplets falling from the woman's face and dousing her blouse. The two spent the remainder of the afternoon planning a small ceremony that would take place on the Puyallup werewolf estate. Halina would be in charge of food, Felicia would take care of the flowers and the three of them would work on the invitations. The planning set Caya's mind at ease as it all seemed like an ordinary wedding. She wanted to wait to discuss the date of the ceremony as well as the particulars of how the actual mating would go with her fiancé once he arrived back home. The term fiancé was going to take some getting used to for sure. They had just finished the initial planning phase when she received the call.

Nick sounded ok and she was sure he could hear the relief in her voice to be hearing his voice. He apologized for not calling sooner. His excuse had been that he had been busy with pack business. She wondered how many times she would hear that excuse during their lifetime together. There it was. She had actually thought it, lifetime together. Surprisingly, it did not frighten her as it once had.

When he asked what she had been doing the last couple of days, she was excited to give him the news of the ceremonial plans that were being made in his absence. Now, it was her turn to hear the relief in his voice. "Are you sure you are ready?" Caya did not hesitate when she confirmed what he hoped to be true. "Yes. I didn't want to admit I missed you, but I hope you are happy now that you drug it out of me. I miss you so much that I am ready to spend the rest of my life with you Nick Wilhelm." He laughed in the phone. "There is my mate with the attitude. Even when I am away you have to come back with your spicy remarks." Caya took her turn to laugh. "I thought my haughty attitude is what you loved the most about me?" Nick continued with their little back and forth. "Well, that may not be all I love about you." Caya took the opportunity to let Nick know that she loved how he was her protector and how he was so patient with her. She really thought he would wait years on her to decide to mate with him if necessary; of course she could also be deluding herself a little bit.

They continued to talk about the decisions that had been made concerning the mating ceremony. Caya was not surprised when Nick asked, "What date have you chosen?" Caya replied, "I thought we would pick a date that would suit your schedule. I know you are busy with the other pack and then when you get home you will need to catch up with your home pack. We can discuss it when you return. I have no schedule so I am flexible."

Nick was not sure how to take this answer. Was Caya stalling or was she just being considerate of his Alpha responsibilities? In addition, there was that part about her not having a schedule. He knew the ceremony was not the only thing they would have to discuss when he returned. They were going to have to talk about her role as his wife and mate. In the meantime, he was going to have to decide if he was willing to allow her to teach, which seemed to be the love of her life at present, a place in her heart that he hoped he would one day replace. He wished he had time to give this thought the needed attention at present, but he had more pressing, immediate issues.

Caya asked how his day went, but she never asked why he hadn't called. Nick did not tell her anything about the fire or about Riker. He did not want her to worry needlessly. However, he was going to have to call Will and warn him to watch for Riker to show up in Puyallup. As soon as word reached Riker that Nick had been chosen by the council to become the Alpha of the Mount Rainier pack, he knew the black wolf would make an appearance to challenge him for the right to be Alpha of both packs. It was common knowledge to those within the werewolf world that if you did not become Alpha through your lineage you could attain that rank by challenging and killing an Alpha. He was sure that Caya did not know about this and this was not something he wanted to discuss with her until it was absolutely necessary. The two mates continued to talk about various things for a little while longer before Caya started yawning and Nick felt exhaustion pulling at his body. He told Caya he would talk to her the next day and to carry on with the wedding plans. Caya much preferred this description to mating plans.

Chapter 19

Will was waiting on Caya in the gym for their evening workout when his phone rang. He looked at the caller ID and saw Nick's name pop up. He answered immediately, knowing that if he was calling something was wrong. He could be inquiring about Caya in light of her attempted abduction, but they had already discussed this so the bodyguard was sure that this call was unrelated to that incident. Nick sounded tired when he said, "Will, I need you to be on the lookout for a jet black wolf from the Mount Rainier pack. His name is Riker Kincaid. He was the Beta of the pack and had hoped to move right into Alpha status with the death of his predecessor. He has gone AWAL after we had a confrontation. He hasn't been seen in two days." Will listened intently while eyeing the door. He hoped Caya took her time to get there because he didn't want her to hear any of this conversation, even just his end of it. Nick continued, "Will, this guy has shown quite the interest in my mate and I am afraid he will come to Puyallup not only to challenge me, but to also lay claim to her."

When his Alpha paused to take a breath, Will joined the conversation. "Don't worry Caya is staying close to home since her close encounter with her former boyfriend. I will keep close tabs on her even here on the estate." He didn't mention that she was a little late for workouts. He didn't want the Alpha to go postal over the phone because he didn't have Caya in his sites at the moment. "I know you will take care of her. That is why I appointed you her protector when I can't be." That comment, even though it was sincere and true, hurt Nick more than he would like to admit. As Alpha, it was his responsibility to protect his mate, but it was also his responsibility to relegate responsibility when necessary as well. He knew that Will and Caya had forged a friendship from the moment Caya arrived in Puyallup and he knew that because of their friendship and Will's loyalty to his Alpha that his loyalty would carry over to his Alpha's mate. If he couldn't be there to keep Caya safe, Will was the best alternative.

Caya walked into the gym just as Will was finishing his conversation. He could feel relief wash over him as she strolled over to him mouthing without sound, "Sorry." Will was actually thankful she was late this time. He was able to finish his phone conversation without her being the wiser as to the topic of conversation. One thing that he had learned about Caya was that once she caught hold of something she would not let go of it until she was satisfied with the resolution. If she knew about Riker, she would be battering him with questions and reassuring him that she could take care of herself. He knew he would have to keep an eye on her because Nick made it clear that this guy was big as in hulky and dangerous. Will also thought he was probably arrogant as that was usually part of the burly male packages he had previously encountered.

His student was already giving him a questioning look. He had to admit she was very cute when she tried to create a serious yet questioning visage with the one lifted eyebrow and intense eye contact. "You are late. Don't think I am cutting your time short tonight because of your tardiness." As Caya headed to the treadmill for her warmup, she said over her shoulder, "Of course not, General. I was only late because I just happen to know you had an important phone call and I didn't want to interrupt your conversation." Will did not miss the smile that appeared on her face. "Likely excuse, it is a shame that you are turning to a world of lying. Your honesty has been so endearing." Will walked over to his own treadmill with a big smile planted on his face. If there was one thing he loved more than wrestling with the she-wolf, it was the banter that they would enjoy most of the time. Keeping things light was what worked for them, and mutual respect. However, he knew that he could not let her call the shots when it came to her safety. He had learned that the hard way. Although, it had turned out ok in the end he knew that his Alpha would not turn a blind eye if something of that magnitude happened to his mate again.

Caya noticed that Will was shadowing her more than normal on the reservation. Usually, when they were home she had a little more privacy. She was attuned to his constant presence and wondered what new danger lurked around the corner. When Will was not with her, grandpa was. He would pretend to have missed her company and would come to have a soda and talk to her about her adjustment to her werewolf life. Caya did enjoy their conversations mainly because he would always impart some type of werewolf lore that she found very fascinating. However, she was still so new at this that he could be filling her knowledge base with pure fiction and she would never even know it. Fact or fiction she still found it fascinating and welcomed his visits. Poor Will needed a break from time to time anyway. Caya was also aware that two and sometimes three other pack members would be a short distance away scoping out the perimeter. She appreciated how considerate Will was not to leave her with those who were unfamiliar to her. Grandpa was the babysitter and the other boys were the protection. She just wondered if Will knew that she had already figured out his strategy. She also had to give grandpa kudos for never mentioning his grandson's attempted kidnapping escapade.

As the revelation of the scenario was unraveling in her mind, she was starting to feel uneasy. The attack by James had come as a surprise to her so she had no time to feel uneasy. She just reacted to the situation as she had been taught. However, this was different. She was starting to become shrouded in dread and suspension, expecting someone to jump out and grab her anytime she walked around a corner. On the one hand this feeling had heightened her awareness of those around her, but she hated knowing fear was consuming her. She was determined not to be taken by surprise again.

By the end of the week, Caya's nerves were frayed. The combination of missing her bond with her mate and the mounting fear that danger was lurking all around her was promising to unravel her. Fortunately for her, a reprieve was imminent. She had fallen asleep in her favorite wing back chair in her library. She was reading and had succumbed to the warmth and softness of the plush chair and with her knees tucked up under her chin had fallen asleep.

Nick entered the house with only one thing on his agenda, finding his mate. He never wanted to let on to Caya how hard it was to be away, to have that bond severed for such a long period of time. In his heart he knew he could wait as long as Caya needed him to wait to complete their bond, but his mind was a total traitor. While he was away, he couldn't make the thoughts subside about how he needed to complete the bond so it could never be severed again and to allay all threats of other male wolves seeking to mate with his chosen one. He ignored the comments of all of those welcoming him back home. No one seemed to mind as they knew well where his thoughts lay at the moment. They managed to give him wide berth to continue his search of the allusive female that was consuming his thoughts. He even bypassed his mother for the first time ever in his life in search of the newest female in his life.

When Nick could not find her in her bedroom, he knew she would be in her sanctuary, the library. He took the stairs two at a time to shorten the distance to his destination. When he entered the room, he stopped abruptly to watch the love of his life who was sleeping so peacefully. He wondered if this was the most peaceful sleep she had encountered since his departure. He knew that he himself had many a sleepless night while he was away. She did not utter a sound, but every few seconds the hands she had wrapped around her up drawn knees would twitch. Her book lay on the floor. He could imagine her fussing because she had not only dropped it on the floor but by the way it was splayed on the floor with pages face down in no apparent order she probably had lost her reading spot. He could tell by the bags under her eyes that she was exhausted. She could probably make out the same bags under his eyes. He didn't have the heart to wake her, but he longed to pull her from the chair and into his arms. It wasn't only the bond he missed, but her smile, her touch, their conversations. There was no doubt that she was his mate because he simply could not live without her in his life. His suspense of waiting on her to wake was short lived. He only had to watch her sleep for a couple of minutes before she started to rouse herself from sleep.

Her eyelids felt like they were made of lead. They were so heavy that it took several attempts before she was able to open them fully. Even though she was successful in opening them, her gaze was not focused. Before she could even see him clearly, she could feel his presence. Feeling the return of their bond aroused her quickly. She was alert and staring right into those emerald gems she had missed for the past week. They gazed into each other's eyes for what could have been seconds but felt like hours before he entered the room. She leapt from the chair and met him halfway. He wrapped those burly arms around her waist and she snaked her arms around his neck, never breaking eye contact. No verbal communication was necessary as their eyes were saying it all. Caya was comforted to have her bond with her mate back in place. The uneasiness she had felt had evaporated once Nick arrived home and into her arms. She felt safe and even loved. After being apart, there was no question that she loved this man and couldn't fathom being without him. He was her lifeline. She was his protector as much as he was hers. Nick finally decided he should commence verbal communication. "So you said on the phone you missed me and now your eyes say you missed me so I have no option but to believe you really did miss me." She was so happy to see his smile again. She had not realized that in just one week she had forgotten how brilliant it was.

Caya's response was immediate. "A girl would never admit such a thing and besides I made an A+ in drama. I intend to keep you guessing as to whether I am acting or sincere." Nick threw his head back and gave the biggest guffaw Caya had ever heard. "Those eyes are way too intense and your response to seeing me to reactive to have been acting when only seconds before you had been in a deep sleep. However, I will give you an A+ for your denial of the fact that you indeed missed me." Caya knew her reaction to him had betrayed her. All she could do was accept defeat. "Well, maybe I did miss you a little." She barely finished her sentence before Nick had planted his lips on hers which betrayed how much he had missed her. This time the kiss lasted several minutes before they parted and she enjoyed every minute that their embrace lasted, although she would never admit that to him.

Chapter 20

Since her mate's return, she and Nick had been almost inseparable. Even though it was nearing Christmas and the weather had turned frigid, they made daily trips to their special place, the lake. Apparently, it was not cold enough to freeze the lake; however, to her disappointment it was too cold for a swim. They sat on the bank and talked about winter, decorating for Christmas, his trip to Mount Rainier, and her near abduction. When the conversation would get too heavy for her, she would steer it to Christmas and the wedding plans. She preferred to refer to this ceremony as a wedding rather than mating ceremony. Nick was willing to appease her in this because he sensed that it made her uncomfortable to discuss mating. He also realized that she didn't want to discuss James at all. She had told Nick that she knew to watch for James and not to think he was willing to leave their relationship to just friendship. She had hoped that he would find his mate and they could remain friends. She may not have been a werewolf for long, but she knew that her relationship with James was causing friction between the Tacoma and Puyallup packs.

She hated that she was the cause of more stress for her mate. He not only had to worry about keeping his pack in line and safe, but also the Mount Rainier pack and he had to worry about the Tacoma pack attacking. The thought of all of this was making her fearful again. She thought Nick was handling everything well, outwardly at least. On the other hand, she wasn't sure she was cut out for all of this conflict and worry. She was amazed to find that she was not as fearful of possible security breaches, but rather whether or not she was capable of defending them and the thought of having to worry about this for this the rest of her life was overwhelming.

One day they were discussing Christmas. Christmas was Caya's favorite time of the year so she couldn't hide her excitement when she asked when they could begin decorating and what types of traditions they had on the reservation to celebrate the festive season. She was comforted by the fact that Puyallup celebrated much like everyone she knew. They had a Christmas tree, lots of food, presents, and apparently Christmas music as Halina had been playing traditional Christmas carols through a speaker system that would play throughout the house.

The new wolf could not contain her excitement when her mate announced they were going in search of the perfect Christmas tree. Caya was use to putting up an artificial tree in her apartment. She had never gone out in the woods and actually cut a tree. She hoped she would not be responsible for making sure it lived through Christmas. She most certainly had no green thumb. Nick had to rein her in a few times when she went from tree to tree and just couldn't make up her mind. He couldn't suppress a laugh when she picked out one that was ten feet high. "Just because we have a twelve foot ceiling doesn't mean we need to carry in a ten foot tree," he admonished. Caya chose to overlook the fact that he was making fun of her and continued in her pursuit of the perfect tree. Eventually, Nick made the final choice and cut the tree.

Caya wondered how they would carry the tree back to the house. "Are you going to change into a wolf and let me strap this tree to your back to get it home?" Nick turned to her with furrowed brow and then his adorable left eyebrow lifted and he responded, "Are you kidding? Seriously Caya, why do you think I brought you? You can change and I will strap it on you. It is common knowledge women have larger hips." Nick knew he had carried that pun a little too far. He was franticly looking around to see what was near her because he knew she was going to throw something at him. Before she could grab a rock or log, they could hear Will's laughter bellowing with the wind through the woods. Apparently, Will thought their conversation was hilarious. When he came into view, he was pulling a sled. That was when it occurred to Caya that Nick had a plan and it involved another back and set of strong hands. Caya just shook her head at both men. They were both having a good laugh at her expense. She chose to ignore them and head toward the house. She had become more astute at relying on her wolf instincts and navigational abilities.

She had not made it far before a set of strong hands grabbed her from behind and turned her around. She was face to face with Nick and he was no longer laughing. "You may be upset because we were laughing, but you cannot just run off on your own!" Will joined them to make sure she was ok. "I figured that you two had this under control and I was headed home. I have learned to find my way around and trust my instincts. Why are you so mad? Your face is blood red." Nick knew he might have overreacted, but he was not letting her out in the woods on her own with other wolf predators that may approach her. "I will explain my overreaction later, but for now you can help get this tree on the sled and into the house. Caya, I am sorry to ruin our fun trip, but I need you to stay close." Caya declined to respond to his comment and headed back to where they had left the tree. By the time they returned home, the mood had lightened and they were ready to decorate the tree.

Decorating the tree as a family was something Caya had missed for many years. Since her parent's accident, she had not had a family to share holidays with her. Rayna was her family and although she enjoyed Nick's family she wished her friend was there to enjoy this time with them. Once the tree was decorated to Halina and Felicia's specifications Nick led Caya out on the balcony of her office.

The air was very chilly, but she had grown to welcome the cold as her body temperature was now hotter due to her physiological makeup. "I wanted to apologize to you about getting mad at you earlier. You didn't do anything wrong. Something happened in Mount Rainier that I have failed to mention to you. It is something that will affect you. I was just waiting for an appropriate time to tell you." Caya was starting to get unnerved. She had no idea what he had left out of his stories about his trip. "The Beta of the Mount Rainier pack, Riker, may challenge me. We did have a confrontation before he ran off and abandoned his pack. It was the night of the fire. We had fought and he ran into the woods. He did not return before or after the fire. Caya, he had learned about my mate. He was often taunting me about how he wished he could find a virgin mate and how he might challenge me and take my mate."

Nick put his hand upon her left cheek and rubbed his thumb across it. "That is why I freaked out when you went off on your own. Now, you have to watch out for James and Riker. I know you do not like having someone babysit you, but honey you have to have someone with you when you leave the house until after the wedding." Caya could see the worry written all over his face. This was not a time for her to rebel. She could not imagine what he had been dealing with while away from her knowing that James and Riker could get to her and do who knows what to her anytime they felt like it. She was not going to rebel, but she could speak her mind about his waiting to tell her about this new threat. "You should have told me before you made it home from Mount Rainier. Did you tell Will? Is that why he has had grandpa and every male you didn't take with you following me around when he couldn't?" Nick simply nodded in affirmation. "I understand that sometimes you must keep things from me that concern the pack, but this concerned me and you still withheld the information. If you really want me to be safe, you have to arm me with information, not just self-defense training." Nick knew she was right. He placed his forehead on her forehead and said, "Touché."

Rayna texted Caya about whether or not she could meet to do some Christmas shopping. She found Nick in his office on the computer. She was very fortunate to find him alone. As she closed the door behind her, Nick's eyes traveled from his computer monitor to her green eyes. He was always intrigued by how Caya's hazel eyes would change from blue to green depending on what she was wearing. His eyes sought her eyes first and then traveled down to see that she was wearing a Christmas green sweater, jeans, and black boots. He was also amazed at how she was always able to coordinate her jewelry with each outfit she wore. Today, she had a gold heart pendent with matching gold heart earrings. The pendent settled right below her collarbone within the v neck of her sweater.

While he was admiring her, she was taking in his appearance as well. She noticed he had chosen to wear a red and black three quarter zip Chaps sweater with his jeans. She thought he was strikingly handsome in the sweater. She had only seen him in his t-shirt and jeans. As she was wondering if he had on his boots or had chosen some other footwear option, he stood and walked around his desk to meet her. Her query was answered when she looked down to see that he indeed had on boots, but these were western type boots not his normal work boots.

"Are you busy? I just needed to discuss a few things with you. I saw you were alone and thought this might be a good time." He smiled as he said, "I will always make time to listen to you. What's up?" He wrapped an arm around her waist and led her to a chair that faced his desk. As she sat in the chair, he perched on the corner of his desk. He could tell this conversation was going to be uncomfortable by the way Caya was fidgeting in her seat. It took her a minute to find the nerve to speak about the issues that were of concern to her.

"Well, Rayna texted and wanted to know if I could meet with her to do some Christmas shopping." Nick wondered if he should make her sweat out his answer, but thought better of it as he thought she most certainly wanted to talk about other serious matters and seemed uncomfortable even without his goading her. "I had hoped you would accompany me shopping today," holding his arms out from him to indicate that he had dressed up for the occasion. "I know you miss your friend. Why don't you take Will and go shop with her this morning and I will meet you around 1:00 for lunch and then you and I can shop a while." Caya thought this to be the perfect solution. She could spend time with both of her favorite people.

"That sounds great. I assume Will and Seth will get their shopping in while we are shopping?" Nick chuckled before adding, "Of course." Caya realized that it was just as dangerous for Nick to be without his bodyguard as it was for her to be without hers right now. She was jealous of how Nick was able to work conflicts out in his head so easily. He was able to come up with a solution without hesitating. It would have taken her at least thirty minutes to have come up with the shopping solution that would benefit everyone involved. She assumed that he was use to making decisions for his pack constantly and was use to making them quickly. She so admired his leadership abilities. He was exactly where he was supposed to be. The question was, was she?

Nick slid his propped leg from the desk to rest his foot on the floor. He was still facing her when he said, "Since that is settled was there something else you wished to discuss?" He had his answer as soon has her face turned pink. She was not good at hiding her emotions. "Yes. I wanted to plead with you to let me tell Rayna about my new life." Before he could give a negative response she continued, "I have known her all of my life and though she will be shocked to hear what I have become, she is like a sister to me and I know she would in no way endanger me by telling anyone. You do not have to give me an answer today. I want you to think about it. Up until I join your family, she is the only family I have and I really want her to be a part of my life and attend my wedding." Nick did ponder her plea a moment before replying, "I want us to tell her together and not in public." Caya didn't know what to say. She thought she would have to wait and continue to plead her case before he told her it would be impossible. She was so stunned that she just sat there with her mouth open staring in disbelief.

Nick smiled, "I take it you were expecting a bigger fight?" She closed her mouth and nodded in consent. She jumped up and clasped her arms around his neck and began to squeeze. When she stepped back and released him, she was all smiles. "You have no idea how happy you have made me," she squealed. "I have an idea given that choke hold you just gave me." He said this as he was rubbing the back of his neck in mock pain, all the while grinning. "Was there anything else on your list of requests for today?" Without returning to her seat, she took on a serious look and continued eye contact with him. "I wanted to have your input about the wedding date. I was wondering if you and the guys could drag yourselves away from the football games to attend a mating ceremony on New Year's Day?"

Nick could see her hands shaking so he placed them into his steady hands. He knew he shouldn't, but it was just their way. "Wow, Caya of all of the days in the year you have chosen the biggest football day of the season to have the wedding." He knew that she would take the bait. She didn't even let him continue. "Well, I can see that it will be a hardship so my next available date will be sometime in June. Every girl dreams of being a June bride." He had no trouble discerning the mischievous twinkle in her eyes. She might seem determined, but her hands, that he still held hostage, were betraying her as they were still shaking and were beginning to sweat. Finally, he relented, "Well considering I would have to wait that long the football games no longer seem so important."

He released her hands and stood before her staring at her eyes as they began to water. He placed a thumb by each of her eyes to wipe away the tears as they began their release. His eyes continued to search her eyes to make sure this was indeed what she wanted. He had his answer as she rose on her tiptoes to place a kiss on his lips. If he had any doubts, she had waylaid them with that kiss. She did not separate after the kiss. She wrapped her arms around his neck again and gave him what was to be his second choke hold for the day. "Thank you, Nick. You have made me the happiest girl in the world. I look forward to starting the year out as your wife."

Once she released him, she started for the door. He grabbed her hand before she was completely out of his reach. "Wait right there. Just because you have all of your answers don't mean that I do not have business with you as well." Caya turned to face him once again a little perplexed. *To what is he referring? Surely, he doesn't expect strings to be attached to my request to let Rayna in on my news.* Nick rounded his desk so quick Caya thought she had imagined the movement. He opened his top, right drawer and pulled out a tiny box. The box was made of purple velvet. He looked a little sheepish as he returned to his place in front of her. "I was going to plan a more romantic proposal, but this feels pretty special right now." Nick got down on one knee as he uttered the words Caya thought she may never hear. "Caya Braswell I have waited to find my mate and you will never know how much joy you have brought to me in the last six months. I won't lie and say that I thought you would never accept me based on the fact that you thought I had kidnapped you. It has taken every ounce of resolve to give you time to adjust to me and werewolf life. I know you are still learning, but now that you are a little more accepting of me will you do me the honor of becoming my wife and forever mate?"

She looked at thc beautiful diamond cut solitaire surrounded by smaller begets along the gold band. She was no longer scared of a possible future with her mate. She knew once their bond had been severed that she would never turn back from him. She never wanted their bond to be severed again. She wanted to rush this ceremony as much as he at the moment. She thought the timing of this proposal was very romantic. She didn't need flowers, music, low lights, or a fancy venue. It was all about their feelings in the moment and he was right to have chosen this moment. "Nick Wilhelm I would be honored to become your wife and forever mate." With that he placed the ring on her finger, rose to wrap her in his arms and they enjoyed another long, passionate kiss that would only mark the beginning of the mating ritual.

They made no announcement to the rest of the household. They went on with their plans for the day. Rayna had noticed the ring immediately and couldn't believe her eyes. Caya was proud of her friend for not questioning her and waiting for Caya to explain. The problem was that Caya couldn't explain anything at the moment. She had made Nick a promise to wait until the three of them were alone to give Rayna the explanation she deserved. The girls shopped until time to meet Nick for lunch. They all ate lunch together and to Rayna's credit she did not give him the cold shoulder. Once they were finished eating and having polite conversation, Nick asked Rayna to join them the following night for dinner at their home. Caya was stunned. She thought he would insist on meeting her at her apartment. Her love for him was only growing as he continued to go out of his way to befriend the woman Caya had adopted as her sister. She only hoped Rayna was as receptive to the news she would soon encounter as Nick was becoming to allowing Rayna into their little realm.

Chapter 21

Nick and Caya announced their engagement at dinner that night. Everyone at the dinner table was ecstatic, especially Halina and Felicia. Felicia kept going on about the wedding plans that you would have thought her to be the bride. Seth gave his adopted brother, Nick, a big slap on the back followed by a man hug. Caya was touched by the genuine emotions that Seth shared with Nick. While Seth was advising Nick to the woes of matrimony, Will came over to whisper his congratulations in her ear. When she turned to thank him, he had an odd look on his face. Before she could discern this look and thank him, he was gone. She thought that to be odd behavior coming from him, but before she could ponder on it anymore other well-wishers were coming to congratulate the couple, apparently word was spreading quicker than a wildfire.

The following evening, Rayna was expected at the house for dinner. Nick could tell Caya was very nervous by her constant pacing from the living room to the kitchen and back to the living room. When she wasn't pacing, she was looking out the window for her friend's car. While she was in the kitchen, Seth asked, "How long are you going to let her wear a path through here?" Nick just looked sideways at his friend. As Caya passed Nick, he reached out and caught her arm and pulled her to him. He whispered in her ear, "You are making the natives nervous. I am the one that should be nervous. We are going to tell this woman, who I do not know, all about our life here in Puyallup. It could be detrimental to my whole pack and you don't see me pacing the floor. You told me we could trust her so why are you so nervous?"

Caya pulled Nick into the kitchen, like that distance matters when you are among werewolves with keen hearing. "I do trust Rayna, but it is not every day that you tell your best friend that you are no longer solely human and from time to time you sprout fur and run on all fours. I am just hoping that my news does not put her into cardiac arrest." Before their conversation could continue, they heard a car. Caya looked out the window and let out a deep breath as she saw her friend exiting the vehicle. She hoped this went well.

Caya took Rayna for a tour of the mansion, as she liked to call it. By the time they were finished with the tour, Halina had dinner ready and everyone was waiting for the girls to join them. Rayna was not as talkative as normal at dinner so Caya discerned some nervousness on her friend's part as well. *Wonder what she would think if she knew she was sitting among wolves?* After dinner, Caya invited Rayna to her library and everyone went their separate ways. Nick gave the girls a few minutes together before joining them in the library. When Caya felt his presence, before he ever entered the room, she asked Rayna to have a seat so that she could share some news with her. Rayna's eyes were very big when Nick walked over to them.

Caya wasn't sure there was an easy way to tell this story so she just commenced and hoped that Rayna could keep up and not pass out. Caya actually started with telling Rayna about James and Lars giving her a blood transfusion after her hiking accident. She went on to tell her that James and Lars were werewolves and that they had saved her life by giving her werewolf blood, which resulted in her becoming a werewolf. She related the story of Nick being her mate and the connection she had felt with him when they saw him that day they were picnicking. To Rayna's credit, she sat there and listened without interrupting once. Caya was certain she must be in shock. When Caya had finished with the announcement of her and Nick's engagement, she waited for Rayna's reply. Caya could sense Nick's uneasiness.

Rayna looked from one to the other before responding. She stood and walked slowly to Caya as not to put Nick on heightened alert, like he wasn't already. She gave her friend a hug and a huge smile and congratulated her. Instead of Rayna being stunned with all of the news, it was Caya who was stunned by Rayna's calm demeanor. Caya new that Nick would have Seth and Will close just in case Rayna was not receptive to the news, but she did expect Rayna to show some signs of surprise. Those signs never materialized. Rayna took one of Caya's hands and one of Nick's hands as she proceeded with her verbal response to this news. "Guys, I knew about the blood transfusion and I knew that James and Lars were werewolves. Caya, I have been dating Lars for more than a year. Don't you think he would have told me about his way of life by now or at the very least something happen to alert me to the fact that he is not all human? While you were recovering, Lars told me about the blood they gave you. He told me not to say a word to you or the news could undermine your recovery. I guess I have known about what you were before you knew what you were."

Caya just about collapsed on the floor. Nick had to catch her to keep her from making contact with the hardwood. Perhaps Caya was the one who should have been seated. She couldn't believe what she was hearing. "You knew that I was a werewolf and you didn't think you needed to tell me! Shouldn't best friends tell each other these things! I understand that you didn't want to undermine my recovery, but why have you not said anything until now?" Rayna replied, "Why haven't you? Lars had told me that you figured it out and were raving mad at James. I told them you would be mad once you knew, but they assured me that there was no other option available to them at the time. I figured you would tell me when you were ready. I have to tell you that it has not been easy for me to not talk about it."

After they talked well into the night, Caya was not as upset with her friend as she had been at the beginning of the conversation. She knew her friend was still looking out for her and letting her get to know herself and then hoping she would open up about what she had become. Before Rayna had left, everything was right with the two friends again and Rayna had consented to be at the wedding and she had also promised not to share information about the Puyallup pack with Lars on the off chance that he decided to share that information with his pack. Caya was pleased that she had crossed this hurdle and could move on with the rest of her wedding plans. She really hoped that as Nick got to know Rayna he would accept that they could trust her. She couldn't imagine starting her new life without her best friend.

Chapter 22

Christmas was nearing and the house was decorated. The tree was lit up with presents underneath. A snow had fallen and when Caya and Nick went for a run the forest looked pure with all of the white snow covering the trees and the ground. Once they returned to their human forms, Caya stood just taking in the beauty of the area. Mount Rainier, in the distance, was snow covered and the sunlight was reflecting off its blanket of snow. Caya couldn't get over how peaceful it was after a snow. The animals were not scurrying around like they usually did, but that may have been because wolves were out and about in the woods.

While Nick was working in his office, Caya decided she would go get a book and some hot chocolate and relax. She had not realized it, but she had been pretty stressed with the James incident, Nick going away, Christmas and wedding preparations, and the revelation that backfired when telling Rayna about what she had become. Rayna had assured her that she was the same person. Now, she was just improved having keen senses and extraordinary strength. She had learned to control her changes with very few exceptions. However, she still had a hard time controlling the change when she was extremely emotional. She was relieved that she didn't have to hide her secret from Rayna any longer and she didn't have to hide her feelings for Nick. She felt like she could relax a little now before the festivities started.

She had found her book and was leaving the kitchen with her cup of hot chocolate with marshmallows with a candy cane in it when she heard a noise outside. She couldn't be sure but she thought it sounded like the whine of an animal. She set her cup and book down on the coffee table and went to the door. She walked out on the front porch. The wind was blowing snow on the front porch furniture. She didn't see anyone, but she heard something at the end of the house. It sounded as though something was digging in the snow. She opened the door back up and grabbed her coat off the coat rack by the door. She felt her senses tingling. She wasn't sure if it was from the cold wind or a warning that danger lingered ahead. She wondered where Will was hanging out because when Nick was not with her Will usually was her shadow. Before turning the corner of the house, she decided it would be best to text Nick. She started the text and just asked him to meet her around the south end of the house.

She rounded the corner of the house and saw a little puppy playing in the snow. It looked like a Dalmatian in reverse. That is to say it was a black puppy with white snow on it where

Dalmatians are white with black spots. She thought it odd that a puppy would hang out among wolves. She tried to approach it, but it would turn and run a few yards and turn back to see if she was following. She would get closer and it would run a little further. She was so focused on the puppy that she totally missed her instincts warning her that she was in danger. That is until she could feel warm breath breathing down her neck. She would have thought it was Nick, but she couldn't feel his presence so he had to still be inside the house. She turned abruptly and lashed out with her right arm. Her arm came in contact with a big, burly arm that was blocking her hit. Her eyes met with a tall, dark and literally handsome man with a large grin on his face.

This guy was very muscular. She couldn't help but stare when she should have been running for her life. She realized who this dark haired giant was just as Nick rounded the corner running and yelling, "Riker!" Riker turned and held up one hand to his aggressor. "I have not laid a hand on her." Nick stopped just short, but Caya found herself on the other side of Riker from Nick. Caya had never seen Nick so mad. She thought he was just a few seconds from turning into his wolf form and attacking this intruder. Keeping his hand raised, Riker added, "Your little mate just tried to attack me. Fortunately for her, I like my women feisty." Caya was letting Riker get under her skin. While his back was turned to her and he was focused on Nick, she took the opportunity to sweep his legs from under him and send him plowing up the snow. Standing over the guy with the big ego, she responded, "The bigger they are the harder they fall. I forget what lesson that was, but I think it was early in my training. By the way, I like my men a little more gentlemanly."

Nick grabbed her left arm and pulled her to him and away from Riker. "Go in the house and call Will to stay with you." Caya just looked at him. "Do it now, Caya!" Seth must have sensed a problem because he came running in search of his Alpha. When he found them, he stopped and watched Riker stand and wipe the snow off his clothes. Seth took his position by Nick. He was flanked on both sides by Caya and Seth. Three against one was not bad odds. Nick pushed Caya behind him while cajoling her by saying, "Please go find Will." *Well that is a little more like it. I don't appreciate being yelled at.* He had never raised his voice to her with such a tone since they had been together. That should have been her clue to get far away because trouble was about to start. Still facing Nick, she started walking backwards to go back in the house as she was instructed. However, it felt wrong for her to leave her mate in imminent danger.

Riker found his voice once more, "There is no reason for her to leave. I am actually here to see both of you." Nick spoke through clenched teeth, "Why are you here, Riker?" Riker just grinned and that grin made Caya stop in her tracks and want to lash out once again at the newcomer. She could tell right away that this was not a friendly visit on his part. "I just wanted to get to know your little virgin mate a little better and since I am here to challenge you for the Puyallup and Mount Rainier packs I figured I would take your mate as well."

Nick sensed his mate's anger and turned just in time to catch her before she went flying with arms swinging at her admirer. By this time, Will had joined the group. Although she was trying to fight her way out of Nick's arms to get at the person who had just tried to claim her in a not so romantic way, Nick was not about to let her go. He handed her off to Will as if she was one of those marshmallows that were probably melted in her hot chocolate by now. "Take her inside," he ordered Will.

Riker started laughing as he commented, "It doesn't look like she takes orders well. She definitely needs someone who will keep her in line." Caya had all she could take. There was no way she would get past Will, Seth, and Nick to get to Riker so she decided a verbal confrontation was better than nothing. "Who do you think you are? There is no way in this life or any other life I would be interested in you. If you think you are the one to keep me in line, you better think again." Riker had that grin across his face again, the one that Caya wanted to smack off his face. She couldn't think of anyone she detested more than the dark haired man before her.

Riker turned his attention back to Nick. "I challenge you to a fight at noon tomorrow." Nick just nodded his head. With Nick's assent, Riker continued his demands. "Caya will be here to watch my domination over you." He looked in Caya's direction. "Once I have taken care of this Alpha, you can have a real Alpha." Nick's face was blood red. Caya sensed more anger in him than she had ever felt generating from their bond. She didn't know how she knew to do it, but she was using their bond and trying to comfort him. It had to be working because he looked at her as if to say, "Thank You." When he faced Riker again, his voice was calm and matter of fact, "Caya is new to this way of life. She has never witnessed a fight to the death. She does not need to witness this one. Allow her to stay inside." Riker laughed, "She doesn't seem very frail to me. This is her way of life now and she will be exposed to it at some point so now is as good a time as any. I want her to be here to congratulate me when I win this battle."

Fight to the death! If Riker has challenged Nick for the two packs and me, does that mean that Riker has to kill Nick to win this fight? Caya was terrified. She was not concerned that Nick would not win, even though Riker did have some height, and weight advantages. His downfall would certainly be his ego. Nick was strong, but he was also smart and intelligence and patience would beat ego any day. She was terrified of having to watch her mate being beaten possibly to near death. Nick responded, "She does not know how to block the bond and she will feel what I am feeling. Do you care so little for someone you wish to take as your mate to make her feel that and allow her to watch it unfold before her?"

"As the challenger, I make the rules. I am allowing this to happen on your land, with your people as witness." Caya couldn't help but to interject, "Well, considering you abandoned your people I guess you do not have a choice in that matter." Once again she had Riker's full attention. She was hoping to get under his skin as he had gotten under hers, but he looked as if he saw her with nothing but admiration. Nick stepped in Riker's view of her as he replied, "You can see that she is willing to fight for me. She will not be able to stay on the sidelines and watch. She will interject herself into the fray and as a result be injured or killed." *Well, I will take that as a compliment. I think he was giving me a compliment anyway. He knows me pretty well come to think of it. I would fight for him. Perhaps he realized this before I did.*

"I am quite certain that your men will keep her in check while we are taking care of business," smirked the challenger. It sickened Caya to know that he thought of this life or death situation as nothing but business. *Surely, Nick doesn't think of this situation as a business transaction. He better not think handing me off to that thug as a business venture. I might get on his nerves some, but even I don't deserve that punishment. Is it possible that if Nick loses that I would have to become Riker's mate?*

Chapter 23

When they returned to the house Nick chose to speak to Seth and Will alone. He assured Caya he would not be long. He knew she would have questions and he told her that he would answer them all as soon as he finished going over some details with the guys. Caya waited not so patiently in the living room. There was no way she would be able to read now, but she did sip her hot chocolate that was just tepid by now. The whole reservation seemed to be a buzz about the challenge that lay before her mate. She could hear the pack members whispering as they walked back to their homes. Caya wondered how many times since becoming Alpha Nick had been challenged like this. She was so overwhelmed with questions and unpleasant thoughts that she started shaking and tears started trailing her cheeks. She was getting frustrated with herself because she had been crying so much lately. It was not like her to cry. She usually took things in stride and faced them head on. That is not to say that she may not have a good cry after the emotional event had been resolved.

Nick spoke with authority to his two friends. He was really just filling them in on how they should keep Caya safe no matter the circumstances. He made it clear to both men that if this confrontation did not end in his favor that Riker should not have access to his mate. Both men asked questions about what they were to do, but they never once questioned his decisions or his authority. When the Alpha felt the plan was well received by all, he dismissed them to rest for the big day. He knew they would have their hands full with Caya. Before Will left the house, Nick called him back to the office as he included his mate in that invitation.

"I just wanted Will to be here so that you know that he is fully aware of what I am about to say to you. We all need to be on the same page." Nick looked between the two members of his audience as he spoke while he explained to Caya her role in this life changing event. Caya listened intently and held her questions at bay until he was ready to receive them. Now, Nick spoke solely to Caya. "Riker has insisted you be present during the challenge, but he never said you actually had to watch the fighting. Therefore, it will be best for you to face Will for the duration of the fight." Caya started to speak, but Nick interrupted her before she was able to utter the first word. "I know that you want to know what is going on, but you are not accustomed to this part of our life. You are too emotionally tied to me to watch what will happen to me during this melee. Fortunately, we have not mated so our bond is not as strong as it will be so you won't actually feel all that I feel, but I am sure you will sense my emotions on a grander scale than you do now even without us having that bond simply due to the fact that my emotions will be stronger during this match of wills and your emotions will be stronger because of the possible outcome."

This all made sense to the new wolf, but she could never imagine how hard it would be to stand on the sidelines while her mate literally fought for his life. Nick continued, "I have instructed Will to take you away from here if I should lose the challenge. By pack law, if Riker wins he will become Alpha of both packs until someone challenges and kills him. I know of nothing that indicates he should take the Alpha's mate to be his mate; however, as a member of this pack you are expected to be a loyal follower of the pack Alpha and to comply with his wishes. I know that you have no interest in becoming Riker's mate and I have no delusions that he will just let you live in peace so it would be best if you and Will went rogue." Nick knew that Will cared for Caya and would keep her safe whether his Alpha ordered him to or not.

Caya looked at Will when she asked, "You are willing to run away with me if the need arises?" Will's look penetrated her heart. He didn't have to verbally answer her question. She and Will had a bond of their own. The bond they had forged was of friendship and mutual respect. Caya felt safe with Will. Nick was right to have chosen him to help her through this way of life and to care for her if he was unable to carry out that task. So that there was no question of his loyalty to her, Will answered her question, "Of course. I will always have your back pain in the butt." He followed that statement with a huge smile that helped put Caya at ease about the situation, if that was possible.

Nick grabbed Will by the shoulder and clasped his hand as Will stood to leave, a show of brotherly love and devout trust. Once Will had left the room, Nick continued forging the getaway plans for Caya. "I need you to pack what you can take in one suit case and put it in your trunk. Will is going to do the same. I have already given him your spare keys. Make sure you have your purse in the trunk and your key in your pocket, along with your cell phone. I have instructed Will to leave as soon as he knows Riker is victor. You should not hesitate; just follow his every instruction to the tee. Can you do that one last thing for me, please?"

Caya stood in front of her mate, eyes locked with his. "You need to concentrate on what you have to do make sure that you are able to carry out our wedding plans and I do not become an orphan of this pack. Although I am familiar with that role, I have grown fond of your pack family and of you. I will do exactly as you have instructed and I will do as Will instructs me. You worry about Nick and let Seth and Will worry about me. I know that as a leader you must have to prepare for the worst, but in my heart I know that I didn't just find a mate to lose him so soon in our relationship. I look forward to annoying you for the rest of our lives." With that she decided to end the conversation and give them what they both needed right now, a loving kiss. She did not intend for this to be the last kiss they had either.

They stood in Nick's office holding one another and just feeling each other's presence without having to utter any words. She knew Nick needed to rest before his confrontation, but she was very reluctant to let go of him. When they did separate, Nick asked, "Do you want to ask me anything?" Caya looked at her boots as she stated, "Please don't leave me." This was not the first time that she had asked this of him. She had asked this after Denae's cruel imagery trick that left Caya devastated to learn that Nick and Denae had been more than just friends. Caya had asked Nick not to leave her when he was consoling her. Nick had wanted to go punish his former girlfriend. He had waited until she was thoroughly comforted then and she knew he would not let her down now. It was important that she exude confidence in her mate now and in that way lend him her strength to do what he had to do.

However, there was one question that she had to have answered. "Nick, you do not consider this challenge with Riker as a business transaction, do you?" Nick looked completely stunned by her question. It was certainly not what he expected her to ask. His brow was furrowed as he looked into her emerald green eyes that matched his and responded, "Of course I don't think of this as business. Someone's life will be taken today and it grieves me to know that it may be by my hand. I know that our ways have not been your ways, but I hope you know me well enough now to know that I am a leader who does what is necessary, but I still have compassion." Caya smiled as she said, "Of course I do. I just wanted to make sure that you still remembered that about yourself." With that they parted so Caya could pack just in case she was forced to flee her home and for Nick to mentally prepare for his battle the following afternoon.

Caya did not sleep and she was sure that Nick had not either. With her thoughts of Denae the previous night, she had conjured an idea that she had to try to execute today before the battle began. So when Riker showed up at noon on the button and everyone had assembled out in the field behind the house, she asked her mate in front of everyone if she could have a few words with Riker before they commenced fighting. Nick was not the only one shocked by Caya's request. Riker even looked perplexed. He was learning very quickly not to underestimate this new wolf. He admired her spunk even if it was not in her best interest to challenge him. Nick looked appalled that she would have such a request. "Please. We will still be in view and he plans on winning me with this display of male aggression anyway; therefore, I am certain he will be on his best behavior." Nick knew that she had asked in front of everyone so that it would be harder for him to deny her request. She could feel his anger breeching the surface of their bond. She chose to think that this would just fuel him for his big win over this egotistical Alpha wanna be. When he looked away from her, she took this to mean go ahead so she started walking away from the crowd with Riker on her heels.

"My, don't you know how to stir up a frenzy," Riker began. Caya turned abruptly on him and stated, "I wanted to see what kind of man you really were because that will tell me what kind of leader you will be should you be elevated to that position someday." She could tell he was overjoyed by his thinking that she had decided that he would be the winner of this power play contest. She had lain awake all night thinking about how this conversation would go and whether or not she would be successful. She was not at all sure she could pull it off, but it was worth a try. She continued her interrogation, "Why do you covet what another has so badly? Would you rather not go start your own wolf pack and search for your true mate rather than accept someone else's cast off?" She hoped her choice of words had not inflamed him to the point that he would not give proper consideration to her questions. From her perspective, he appeared more entertained by her questions than infuriated by them. He placed that arrogant grin on his face that she so loathed which was indication to her that he was willing to continue with the game she had instigated.

"My little wolf cub, you have so much yet to learn about our way of life. One does not just move to a remote location and invite guests to join him in his commune for the sole purpose of creating his own wolf pack. A perspective Alpha must prove himself to be worthy of such a role and eliminating the competition is how one moves up the hierarchy. It is very strategic for me to choose to challenge an Alpha that is the leader of two well established packs. Why settle being the leader of one pack when you can have two?" Caya had to admit his plan was well thought out. He was nothing if not power hungry. Before she could put that thought into words, he continued, "As for not searching for my own mate, I have to say that I am so intrigued by you that I believe we could develop a mating bond with no trouble whatsoever."

"What exactly intrigues you about me, Riker?" Riker chuckled at her increasing curiosity. "Most females prefer to remain subdued. They just follow the lead of their mates and do what he asks of them and nothing more. You, on the other hand, seem to forge your own place in this pack and you are not afraid to speak up even to the Alpha when you have strong conviction. I am curious, did you possess these characteristics before you became a werewolf or is this a product of your transformation?" Now it was Riker's turn to make her reflect on herself. All of this time she was afraid that by becoming a werewolf she was losing herself, but this total stranger who had very little interaction with her had already established that she was who she had always been and becoming a werewolf had not kept her from being true to herself. Halina and Rayna were right. She was still the same Caya Braswell she had always been just with a few enhancements.

Once this revelation was made she felt such relief sweep through her consciousness. However, she had to continue with her plan of giving Riker his own revelation. "Why did you leave the Mount Rainier pack? Weren't you already in line to take over as Alpha for that pack?

All you had to do was show them that you had what it takes to move from Beta status to Alpha status. If you had welcomed Nick, and tried to forge a friendship with him and worked with him your own pack would have trusted you to lead them. Instead you left them when their commune caught fire and you fled from a confrontation with an established Alpha. Even if you win this competition, what makes you think you will gain the respect of either of these packs or even my respect for that matter?"

Caya could tell Riker was growing wearisome with this conversation and by Nick's pacing she was only delaying the inevitable. "I may have a mate waiting for me somewhere, but right now I have my eye on you. I have taken a fancy to you Miss Braswell and as to your idea of what creates respect, don't delude yourself. By killing an Alpha, I will command all respect, even from you." With that statement, Riker turned and walked back to face his opponent and Caya felt deflated. She had hoped to be able to connect to Riker's compassionate side, but she now knew that he did not have one. Before Riker was out of ear shot, she had to lend him one more tidbit of truth. "Riker, I am afraid arrogance will one day be your downfall." Riker stopped in his tracks, but did not turn to face her when he replied, "That may be true, but it won't be today my little mediator." She just watched as he walked further and further away from her and toward his possible demise.

Chapter 24

Caya took her place in front of Will. He went ahead and wrapped his arms around her without making her face him. She was not sure if this was to comfort or restrain her. She guessed that it was both. She couldn't take her eyes off of her mate as he removed his shirt in preparation for this battle. She wasn't sure whether they would fight in human or wolf form, perhaps both. When he made eye contact with her, she broke free from Will and ran to him. She placed a kiss on his cheek and whispered, "I love you and always will. You have this and I am not the least bit worried." With her infectious grin placed on her visage, she added, "Be safe." He came back with a grin of his own and his standard reply, "Always." As she left him to take her place with her current protector, Nick added, "I love you and always will." She couldn't help but smile and look up to the beautiful snow free sky, to the sun that illuminated their world today and prophesized, "Love trumps arrogance." With that statement, she resumed her spot with Will. Riker pretended not to have heard her revelation. He would not take her bait. He would merely prove he was the better choice to be her leader.

The two men changed before her eyes into their wolf forms. Apparently, if you wished to lead a wolf pack, you fought as a wolf. The brown wolf allowed the black wolf the first attack. Caya was not sure if this was common wolf courtesy during a fight or if it was just Nick's way to strike with self-defense as his purpose rather than just a killing instinct. The black wolf lunged at the brown wolf and narrowly missed his mark as the brown wolf fainted to the left and quickly turned so his flank was not unprotected. Nick continued to stand his ground, but not to seem to be the aggressor. Will added commentary for Caya's benefit. "Nick is sizing up his opponent. He is trying to determine his strengths and weaknesses. This is not Nick's first challenge. He can hold his own with Riker, princess. *Princess! What happened to "Pain in the Butt?* Will did not distract her attention for long. She continued to watch the two wolves parry and size each other up.

The black wolf tried to take the advantage again and this time he was able to get his wide snout into the brown wolf's flesh. With the wolf's yelp of pain, Caya took that as her que to stop watching the fray. As she was turning to place her forehead into Will's chest, he assisted her momentum and wrapped her tightly against him.

The brown wolf ignored his pain and took the opportunity to launch his own attack on the black wolf's midsection. To the black wolf's credit, he winced in pain but didn't utter a sound other than a growl at his aggressor. Caya knew that instinct would control this match since the two were in wolf form. She knew this from her own experience with changing to wolf form. Her wolf was in control when in animal form. However, she had been told by Nick on occasion that those who were born as a wolf had years of experience becoming one with their wolves and they relied on wolf instinct, but also human reason. The combination made them deadly. Unfortunately, that would be evident today.

Caya could not tell the difference between yelps once they both started acknowledging their pain, but she could feel Will's grip tighten on her with his reaction that she assumed to be another attack on her mate. The two wolves were circling each other and the brown wolf noticed that the black wolf was trying to keep his good side to his opponent. The brown wolf had to create a situation where he could attack the wounded side again and then go for the legs to make the challenger's attacks slower. They circled several times before the brown wolf launched himself at the black wolf's foreleg. His jaws latched on and he was relentless in tearing flesh and crunching bone. The problem with this maneuver was that it left the brown wolf's body unprotected in the vicinity of the black wolf's snout full of bared, knife like teeth, which found their mark in the Alpha's upper back.

Caya covered her ears at the howling of pain that was coming from both wolves. She was not aware that she was shaking until she felt Will's grip slacken and he started rubbing his hands up and down her arms as if he thought she were chilled and was trying to warm her. She was amazed at how attuned he was to her every reaction and still focused on his Alpha fighting for his life. She kept her ears covered with her hands and her eyes shut tight. She could still hear wailing through the protection of her hands and she could still feel the sheer determination of her mate forcing its way through their bond.

The two wolves had separated as if to get their second wind before continuing the brutal attacks. It was the black wolf that took the initiative and head butted the brown wolf in the ribs. The sheer force sent the brown wolf up in the air to land several feet away from his opponent. Before Caya's mate could regain his breath, the aggressor continued the onslaught and attacked the weakened Alpha's foreleg. The quick thinking Alpha took the opportunity of having his foe in such close proximity to his mouth and he caught the black wolf by the nape of the neck and relentlessly set his teeth in and tore hunks of flesh and hair from the once handsomely sleek black dominator. It was time for the Alpha to get the upper hand in this fight.

As the black wolf instinctively tried to pull his body from the wolf's chops, he was helping to tear his own flesh even further. The ebony fighter continued to bite hard on the leg of his opponent and eventually the brown wolf released the black wolf from the throngs of his jaws.

Both wolves panted and it was sheer determination that forced the brown wolf up on three legs and into the neck of the black wolf. The Alpha showed his dominance as he tore the throat of his aggressor and ended the battle. The black wolf twitched for a few minutes with everyone looking on in anticipation before succumbing to his injuries. The brown wolf collapsed from exhaustion before he could make it back hopping along on three legs to reach his mate.

Will kissed the top of Caya's head just before he turned her to face the battlefield. She saw both wolves prostrate on the ground and started a panicked wheezing. Will leaned down and whispered in her ear, "Look for breathing." With that bit of advice, her eyes searched the body of her mate and she was relieved to see that his torso was moving with each intake and exhale of breath. She ran to him and fell on her knees beside him. She was so overcome by his wounds that she couldn't help but start crying. She wanted to touch him, but couldn't find an area on his body that wasn't injured. Will was by her side and Seth was opposite her at their Alpha's side. She could barely hear Will speaking to her through her sobs. "He is too exhausted to change forms. The longer he stays in wolf form the quicker he will heal."

Men were already moving the carcass of the dead wolf. Although Caya was relieved that her mate was alive she still had compassion for the dead. She wished there had been an amicable resolution to this conflict, but she was keenly aware that when dealing with different personalities and backgrounds one could never be assured of an amicable resolution. She knew it was always best to try to search for one before resorting to violence, but sometimes one had to defend himself regardless of the situation.

Caya was told that werewolves heal at a rapid pace, but once the good doctor arrived to attend her mate's wounds she felt even more peace that he would heal. He had remained unconscious for hours. Will explained that his pain was so great that his body was coping by keeping him unconscious. Once the big green gems of the wolf appeared, Nick started changing into his human form. His friends carried him by handmade stretcher into the kitchen and laid the stretcher on the kitchen table where the doctor tended his wounded body. Fortunately, the bone in his leg had not broken through and once set could heal properly. The doctor had to do that while Nick was in wolf form because of the rapid rate of healing that he would undergo. The doctor wanted the leg to heal properly so it was imperative to set the leg immediately. The rest of his wounds could be cleaned and bandaged easier once he was in human form.

Will did not let Caya go to the kitchen until the doctor was finished with her mate. Caya wanted to be with Nick and she resented her bodyguard for not letting her be near him. He kept reminding her that the doctor had to have room to work and if Nick were at the doctor's office she would not be allowed in the room while the doctor worked. That did little to allay her frustration. Finally, the doctor came out and Caya was allowed in to see her mate. He did look a little better now that he was in human form, clean, and bandaged. However, he was still a gruesome sight to behold. He was conscious and tried to give her a little smile. It was evident that exhaustion was overtaking him and he would be a sleep before long. The doctor had given him antibiotics to help prevent infection, but pain medicine was a waste as his body temperature would burn the medicine off too quickly to be of any benefit.

When they thought he could stand to be moved, the guys carried him up to his room. Caya had never been in his room. His room was painted with beige walls and the baseboards were oak stained. There were very few items adorning the walls. His bedding was a chocolate and cream patchwork design. It looked very manly. It felt very intimate being inside his room and very uncomfortable with other people in the room with them. Once he was settled in his own bed, everyone left the room to give them some privacy. He opened his eyes and said, "I didn't leave you," before drifting off to sleep. Caya just grinned in knowing agreement to his observation.

Chapter 25

Although Nick was not one hundred percent the next day for the Christmas activities, he was well enough to participate by eating and opening presents. His ribs were still pretty sore so he couldn't sing Christmas carols, but he enjoyed listening to them. Halina forced all of the guys to participate whether they could blend their voices or not. It ended up sounding very melodious.

Caya had been waiting on Nick like he was an invalid. Eventually, Seth reprimanded her and told her she was spoiling him. After a few more days, Seth was convinced Nick was healed, but refused to let on so that Caya would continue to baby him.

Nick was anxious to get back to leading the pack from his office rather than his bedroom. Caya was taking such good care of him that he wanted for nothing. Before he could even ask, she was there with whatever she had perceived he needed. He was starting to question whether or not the bond was fully functional without the mating. As the wedding day drew near, Caya began to spend more of her time attending wedding plans rather than attending Nick so he was forced to get back into his daily routine. His mother seemed a little stressed about having enough food, but Caya seemed to be taking everything in stride.

Nick was fully recovered by the day of the mating ceremony. Caya insisted that he not see her for breakfast so Felicia delivered her meager breakfast to her room where she was sequestered until time for the ceremony. Nick knew that not seeing the bride before the ceremony was a human ritual, but he intended to placate his mate, at least for this one day. He had planned on taking her somewhere after the ceremony, but she insisted that he needed to rest after his battle with Riker and he had to focus on governing the two wolf packs that were in his care. He knew she would not be content to stay at home for long so he would get to take her somewhere soon.

The house was still decorated for Christmas and that was how Caya had wanted it decorated for the ceremony and considering her favorite time of the year was Christmas, she found it to be perfect. She was no longer nervous about how the mating would go. She just trusted Nick's explanation that instinct would take over. He had never been with his mate so how he knew this information was beyond her. Tonight was to be a full moon which was the perfect time for the mating ceremony, or so she was told.

An elder from the Mount Rainier pack had agreed to perform the ceremony and to include parts of a wedding ceremony as well. Apparently, Nick had arranged this while he was on the mountain and all he had to do was call the elder with the day and time once they had made a decision. Right before the ceremony commenced it began to snow. Caya was looking out her bedroom window and reflected on how it was appropriate to set the mood for their special day. It symbolized the purity of the love that they had found with one another. Before the guests arrived, Halina had whisked Caya off to her library so that she could walk down the stairs to meet her mate before the elder began the rituals. Halina and Felicia were helping her get her wedding dress over her recently coiffed hair and they were all giggling at the spectacle that was taking place to get the job completed.

Once the bride was dressed, Caya felt very emotional. She was trying not to cry because she didn't want her makeup to run all down her face. However, she insisted on letting these two beautiful women inside and out know how much she appreciated them making her a part of their family. She approached Felicia while Rayna was putting the last touches on her wedding bouquet. "Felicia, I have always wanted a sister. Up until now Rayna has been the sister I adopted. I am very blessed to have another sister now. Thank you so much for welcoming me into your family." Felicia gave her a big hug and said, "I have waited a long time to have a sister. You wouldn't believe how bothersome it is to have a brother." They all giggled at her joke. Caya interjected, "Just remember I love that brother of yours." Felicia countered with, "I will remind of you that when he becomes bothersome to you." That comment garnered a few more chuckles from the group.

Caya hugged Halina next. "Halina, I have longed to have a mother again and I can't think of anyone to fill that role besides you. I appreciate how you not only accepted that role, but played the role without ever being asked. You have never treated me any way other than your own daughter and for that I will always love you." Halina returned the hug with tears in her eyes. "Now, you are making my makeup run. Caya, you make me so happy and you fit into this family like the missing piece to a puzzle. I admire the strength you have shown in the difficult days you have had recently. You have weathered them and come out of them stronger than ever. Not only do you make the family happy, but most importantly you make my son happy and for that I will always love you.

Caya had a special message for Rayna as well. "Rayna, you have been my adopted sister ever since I lost my own family. You have always laughed with me in times of joy and you have always picked me up when I was down. I hope you know how much I love you and appreciate your loyalty to me even when it seemed I was being guided away from you." Rayna hugged her bestie and replied, "What are friends for!" After this exchange, each woman surrounded Caya and they all participated in one big group hug with watery eyes to accompany it.

When Caya heard the wedding march, it was her que to start down the stairs. She was so excited to finally have reached this milestone in her life that she wanted to take the stairs two at a time, but she was afraid she would have a misstep and fall flat on her face. Nick would never let her live that down so she proceeded with caution. When she reached the foot of the stairs she saw her dashing mate dressed in a tuxedo, as was the wedding custom. She had picked out a gray tux with a lavender cumber bund and bow tie. He looked a little uncomfortable but was willing to do this for her on this special day. He wasn't the only one that seemed uncomfortable in a tux. Seth and Will carried themselves as if they were afraid to move in their wardrobe. The women who stood up for Caya were dressed in shin length lavender, satin dresses. You would never know that lavender was the bride's favorite color. The bride wore a simple white satin dress that hugged her body, her chest and arms covered in white lace. She carried a white bouquet of roses with sprinkles of lavender painted baby's breath and greenery. Nick could not take his eyes off of his mate as she descended down the stairs.

The ceremony was a blend of wedding and mating rituals. The couple was happy that it went on without any obstacles. This had to be the first event that went without some catastrophic event since they had met. After the ceremony, everyone was eager to partake of the home cooked meal that had been prepared by Halina and her entourage. After they had finished eating, Caya was speaking to some members of the pack and thanking them for attending the ceremony. She was surprised when Nick had walked up behind her as quiet as a mouse and wrapped his arms around her. She turned her head to face him just in time to receive a kiss. She felt his smile warm her as the fire would have if she were sitting nearby. He was there to announce it was time to open wedding gifts. People packed the house standing in the hallway, just outside the kitchen, and all around the living room. Caya and Nick sat in the middle of the pack and opened one gift after another.

She thanked each individual as she opened each gift and would make a remark about how she could best use the item. They received glass bowls, picture frames, picture albums, cooking utensils, and bedding and bath items. She was down to the last gift when that familiar tingling swept over her. She reluctantly opened the gift with much goading from her husband. He couldn't help but tease her about how quickly she had opened the other gifts and the fact it was taking her twice as long with this one. Once she opened the rectangular box, she found a typed note. The note read:

> **Things are never as they seem and there are no happy endings.**

Underneath the note, Caya found a painting of two wolves, both brown, by a lake and the painting had been cut in half as to leave the two wolves separated.

Printed in the United States
By Bookmasters